# Venomous Minds

# 2

## Poison

## Running

## Free

## Nichole Martin

VENOMOUS MINDS 2: POISON RUNNING FREE

Printed in the United States of America

ISBN-13:978-0692397800

ISBN-10:0692397809


Printed by Createspace 2015

Published by BlaqRayn Publishing Plus 2015

*www.smilesforthefuture1.com*


POISON RUNNING FREE

# Venomous Minds

## 2

Poison

Running

Free

## Nichole Martin

# Prologue

"Great, we're finally here," I said. He and his friend began to laugh. "Why you so hahpee (happy) - you didn't drive any," his Grenadian reminded me.

"Still, I didn't have fun ridin' in the back either. It was HOT back there!" They laughed as if that shit was funny. Ha! Ha! My ass – it was really hot back there! He dropped the friend off at a girlfriend's apartment and afterwards we headed for our temporary dwelling place.

Teddy had arranged for us to stay at a friend's house. It was gorgeous - big backyard, pool - the works.

"Hey Clark, what's up muhn?" Teddy greeted his friend as they shook hands.

"Teddy. Glad you two made it here safely. You two have a seat while I go tell my wife that you guys finally made it, because she was asking about you all."

"Okay," Teddy acknowledged his friend. Moments later Clark re-entered the living room with his wife.

"Teddy....Nishi. This is my wife Janette."

"Hello," Teddy and I spoke simultaneously.

"You guys must be really tired. How long was the trip?" Janette asked.

"Ninetin hours," Teddy answered.

"Oh you guys did well." Janette responded in amazement.

"So Nishi, did you drive also?" Clark inquired.

"No, not coming, but I'm gonna help out going back."

"Are you serious? Can you handle that big van?" Clark asked, questioning my skills.

"Yeah," I said as I smiled.

POISON RUNNING FREE

"She drives a vahn like me own back in New York," Teddy bragged.

"So you two are the perfect couple – ehh?" Clark added.

"Yeah muhn!" Teddy said as he turned and looked at me with the biggest smile that someone could ever have.

"I'm sure you two wanna shower and relax now, so Teddy here's an extra set of keys if you should go out," Clark said.

"Alright – t'anks (thanks)." Teddy took the keys.

"We're going to be stepping out for a while so make yourselves at home." Janette and Clark were a nice couple with two children and a beautiful home. They seemed to be extremely happy with one another - like the Cosby's.

"Nishi open dee doe (door!)" Teddy hollered while I showered. Obviously, he had attempted to enter the bathroom, but the door was locked.

"Wait! Just wait until I get out!" I yelled back.

"But I have to piss!" he pressed.

"You hold it! I'm getting out soon."

"I have to piss now!" He was acting like a little boy. I quickly dried off, got dressed and opened the door. There he stood tall, slim and hairy.

"Why are you looking at me like that? I thought you had to use the toilet?" He sucked his teeth then walked into the bathroom. I heard him mumble something about not being fair. Whatever!

The movie "Batman" had just come out and it was also now showing in Florida. So after a bite to eat, he purchases tickets for the next showing.

POISON RUNNING FREE

"The movie doesn't stat (start) until 6:00 so let me call me brudda (brother) to let him know that I'm here."

"Call your brother?" I became suspicious.

"Yeah - he said that I should call him when I rich (reach) down haye (here)." We had about twenty minutes to spare until the movie started, so I took a seat near the water fountain and patiently waited. About fifteen minutes into his call, I grew a bit concerned about us making it back to the theater in time.

"Teddy!" I called over to him. Immediately, he raised his index finger to his mouth, gesturing that I should be quiet then buried his head deeper into the booth. At that point, I walked over to him.

"Shush? Why do I have to be quiet? The movie is about to start," I told him.

"Shush!" The ass wipe did it again. What? Who are you telling to be quiet?

"Sssssssst......who the hell are you SHUSHIN'?" I asked in an angry tone. Instead of him shushing me again, he was now fanning me away. Oh hell no! I backed off and walked back over to where I had been sitting. By the time I had returned to the water fountain he had hung up and was walking towards me.

"Who were you talking to?" I questioned him as he approached me.

"Me brudda! I told you that I was calling me brudda," he reiterated.

"You're a liar! If that really WAS your damn brother, then why were you telling me to be quiet?"

"Because I couldn't hear what he was saying."

POISON RUNNING FREE

"You're such a damn liar. You were talking to MooMoo weren't you?" For a moment he didn't say anything.

"No." He looked away.

"Forget you man. I'm so tired of your shit. You make me sick." Teddy wasn't the type to argue, so in order for him to shut me up – he simply walked away. I grabbed his ass.

"Gyurl, get off of me. Don't be pulling on me," he said, snatching away from me. I could see that he was getting annoyed so I left him alone. In the theater we sat next to each other, but leaned in the opposite directions. Half way through the movie he stood up.

"Let's go!"

"But the movie isn't finished yet," I argued.

"It's boring and I'm not in the mood." Forget you fool. You're just mad because I know that it was really MooMoo on the phone. By the time we got home we were both hot and sticky again.

"Do you wanna take a shower first or what?" I asked him.

"You go fuss (first)," he said. After showering, we laid in bed with our backs facing one another.

Sometime during the early morning hours he rolled over and hugged me.

"Nishi - are you slippin' (sleeping)?" he whispered.

"Nope - you heartless asshole! You have a serious problem."

"Are you still mad at me? I didn't want to tell you that it was she who was on dee phone, because I knew that you would have gotten upset."

POISON RUNNING FREE

"Whatever!" I threw up my hand as if to say that I didn't want to hear it.

"Please don't be upset with me?" he begged.

"You lied – as usual. You told me that you were calling your brother. How did we go from your brother to MooMoo?"

"I did call me brudda - but nobody was home. I had to call somebody to say I made it haye (here) okay."

"And that somebody had to be MooMoo right?" I raised my left brow. Teddy didn't respond, but what he did do was run his hand up the back of my leg, slide down my panties and slightly pried my legs apart. Gently, he began to kiss me as he massaged my body. I slowly turned to face him and removed my right arm from beneath the sheet.

"Take your damn hands off of me!" Again, raising my left eyebrow, I mushed him in his face.

"Did you think that you're basic sweet talking bull was gonna get you a piece of this ass?" I sneered, yanking my panties back up. Your shit aint wuckin (working) haye (here) brudda (brother).

At the first sign of sunlight, we showered and prepared to follow through with his true purpose for visiting Florida; Mr. Habitual had to re-up on his Visa. Florida's I.N.S., (I)ndividuals (N)ot (S)traight building, was like being at the Labor Day Parade in Brooklyn. The only difference was that the foreigners weren't jumping up nor waving their hands or flags in the air because they were too busy thinking about if their applications would be approved or not – the thought of being deported was heavily on their minds. Despite the fact that there were hundreds of applicants, Teddy was in and out. Hmmm....I wonder if he only took me along just in case he needed to get married right away...

*"BELIEVE IN YOURSELF"*

*SITTING AROUND THINKING OF SUCCESS*

*WHY IN HELL IS MY LIFE ONE BIG MESS*

*ALWAYS TRYING' A WAY THAT IS RIGHT*

*STILL I'M STRUGGLING BUT PUTTING UP A FIGHT*

*CHANGE IN MY POCKET BUT I DON'T CARE*

*IT HURTS TO VIEW MYSELF IN THE MIRROR*

*WHEN THE REFLECTION HAS NO GLARE*

Of course, when we returned home, I didn't see him for several weeks. No problem, because a new semester was about to start again and I didn't have time for his craziness. Registration and the preparation of the new school route kept me busy – as usual. I received my Pell and Tap checks early this semester, and being that my mother's new van was a stock one, I utilized that money to style it up a little. With those funds I tinted the entire van and upgraded the sound system - the factory one kept eating up the cassettes. Every time you turn around a tape was tangled in the head and THAT, we couldn't have because then Lee wouldn't have been able to hear his favorite Reggae song – Life Is What You Make It by Frighty and Colonel Mite. He always sang along, very loudly might I add, each time I'd play it.

At the beginning of the song, only the instruments would only be playing. Shortly thereafter, the D.J. would come on and say, "ALRIGHT! ALRIGHT! LICK WOOD MEANS REWIND AND THE GUN SHOT MEANS FORWARD. YOU REQUESTED IT - SO WE REWIND WIND - WIND – WIND." Then the D.J. would play the song again.

POISON RUNNING FREE

Before purchasing the radio, I asked my mother if she would help out with the upgrading. Her response: she didn't have the money because she was now making payments on a vehicle; however she wanted the tints and radio just as much as I did. So without her assistance, I took complete control of the upgrading, knowing that my contribution was greatly appreciated.

I kept this van looking good – inside AND out. I'd wash beneath it with my bare hands to free it of its never ending accumulating grit and tar. I took pride in what I drove and the entire Brooklyn borough recognized this. I remember one midwinter morning, a passerby saw me washing the van.

"Damn ...its 15° below out here and you're washing a van ...??? You GOTS to be crazy!" He bellowed from the front of the driveway. I laughed him off and continued scrubbing.

In addition to studying, term papers and my mother's business, I had recently become a member of the O.E.S. (Order of the Eastern Star). Where did I find time for all this? Beats me.

HUNK! HUNK! HUN-N-NK! (Horns blowing)

While sitting at a red light with a van full of school kids, my head began to spin and I felt as if I was about to faint. Kids were screaming and I had no idea why I was even there. Drivers behind me angrily blew their horns while I sat in a daze at the green light. It was one big chaotic scene. This episode didn't only happen once. I

POISON RUNNING FREE

experienced these same symptoms at home, but thank God this time I fell against the kitchen cabinets. Luckily for me, Grams walked in and helped me to a chair.

My mother was informed and a doctor's appointment was made. A CAT scan, blood work and electrocardiogram were all performed. About a week later during my follow–up visit, the doctor entered the room with all of my results.

"Ms. Maron, your daughter obviously has a lot going on in her life, because her results indicate that her body and mind are undergoing a lot. This, of course, can cause any individual who's experiencing too much stress to shut down at any time."

"Nishelle what do you do?" He asked me.

"I'm a full time student and I drive school kids," I answered.

"Whewww! The school children alone will do it," he jokingly stated.

"But seriously speaking, whatever you're doing it has to stop or you'll find yourself in the hospital." My mother and I looked at each other.

"I can give you something that will relax you, but if you're going to continue living the same lifestyle - then it's useless," he added.

"Write the prescription." I ordered.

"Okay, but remember what I said. By the way, what's your major?" he asked.

"Dental Hygiene," I replied.

"Wow! I remember those days and long nights of studying. School alone requires much dedication and you will burn out eventually, if you don't slow down."

POISON RUNNING FREE

My mother drove us home that day. *No matter what I do, I gotta finish school* I kept repeating in my head. This school bus driving thing wasn't for me.

"Mommy you're gonna have to find somebody else to drive the van for you `cause I'm not giving up college." I could tell by the look on her face that she was between a rock and a hard place, but this time I couldn't help her.

"Nish, I don't know what I'm gonna do. I have all these kids, & what am I supposed to tell the parents? That I'm going out of business because I have no driver?" she complained.

"I don't know what you gonna do. All I know is that you're gonna have to do it quick."

For the next month or so, I continued to drive, hoping that she'd find someone soon but no such luck. I grew very impatient.

VENOMOUS MINDS 2

"Mommy, so what's the deal with a driver?" I asked.

"I'm still looking. There's this one guy that I was thinking about, but I hear he's on crack now. So he's out."

"Put an ad in the paper or something," I suggested.

"Nishi, PLEASE! Can I have just ANYBODY drivin' my van? No! I can't. If I have to, I'll just get rid of the business."

I hated to see my mother in a jam like this, but what was I to do? It was either me and school or me and the business, and as far as I was concerned, the business had to go. Shit, it wasn't like I was getting paid for it anyway. She needed to understand that SCHOOL was my priority.

"Nish." My mother flatly called my name as she entered my room. "When you're done studying let me know `cause I wanna talk to you about somethin'."

POISON RUNNING FREE

I nodded my head as she slowly closed my bedroom door. Within seconds, I got up and moved my papers to the side. I can proofread this later; let me see what she wants.

"What's going on?" I asked as I took a seat on the edge of her bed.

"You know that I'm having a hard time finding a driver, so what I was thinking is that maybe you could take a break from school and......"

"STOP SCHOOL?!" I loudly interrupted.

"Just for a little while."

"I can't do that. I want to finish and finish within the next six years not twenty," I explained.

"Nishi, wait. You didn't let me finish. If you do the run for me I'll pay off all your credit cards and buy you a car." She offered.

"But Mommy when will I finish school?"

VENOMOUS MINDS 2

"I said if you take a little break from school, then maybe you can go back within a year or so. Well - after you get some rest."

"Ohhh - so you're sayin' that your business is more important than my education?"

"No, that's not what I'm saying Nishi. What I'm sayin' is that you need to rest RIGHT? And I need a driver, so look at it this way - we'll be helping each other out. Come on now...you know I'll hook you up. I'll take care of you now and I know that you'll take good care of your mother when you get older and finish school. So do we have a deal?" She rubbed my back.

That following week, I withdrew from each and of my classes. Both my lab and Medical Terminology professors were disappointed when I told them that I would be leaving. They weren't the only ones either – my uncle Wasobi (Evelyn's husband) thought I was making the worst

POISON RUNNING FREE

decision of my life. Because the withdrawal period had officially ended, I was hoping that the school didn't bill me or request a percentage of my Pell and Tap grants back; that money was already spent. As for my mother offering to pay off my credit cards, she shouldn't have even mentioned that because she was the one that ran them up to begin with.

Like a fool, I applied for, and received, every credit card the college had to offer. Little did I know it would haunt me later. My mother's credit was shot to the point where she couldn't even have a phone line in her name, so when she asked me if she could use them to buy Jivasti some new equipment for his band, I agreed.

"As long as you make the payments," I told her. The minimum payment was only $10 a month. Usually I received my bills at the beginning of each month.

*******

VENOMOUS MINDS 2

"Mommy …my credit card bill came and it's due on the 17th."

"I'll give it to you at the end of this week after all the parents have paid," she said, but when the end of that week came, it passed and a new week had begun. I didn't want to be a nuisance, but the bill had to get paid.

"Mommy, umm…I asked you last week about the $10 for my credit card payment, but you never gave it to me and it's due on the 17th, which just so happens to be next Saturday." It was already the 11th and I couldn't understand why she'd wait until the last minute.

"When Billy's mother pays you tomorrow morning, take $10 out from that." She had the nerve to respond with an attitude. Whatever!

Getting her to make those payments was like pulling teeth. She made, or should I say I made, the $10 payments for the next several months, but what was a $10

POISON RUNNING FREE

payment on a $500.00 bill? AND to add insult to injury, remember the carfare allowance? Well, even THAT was no longer being given to me. For what? I was now a college dropout and didn't need it. Or any money if I left it up to her.

"Nish, don't worry," Mom said. "Cause once I get on my feet and finish paying off this van, I'll hook you up."

Does deja vu ring a bell? For the next two years I drove that van for my mother for FREE! Not a single damned dollar! Ni un centavo!

Renee's daughter was about two years old now. Yep, she had a girl and I took care of her as if she were my own. For some reason, I felt as though I had to give that little girl my all because of my past.

I remember one night when Teddy paid me a visit.

VENOMOUS MINDS 2

"Gyurl, that's you baby gyurl! Renee can forget about it!" he exclaimed.

"Why do you say that?" I replied.

"Because every time I see you, I see she. She's always on the run wid you. Look! She haye wid you now and as usual eating french fries."

"Be quiet," I laughed.

Teddy had no knowledge of my prior pregnancies and/or abortions, so he had no inkling why I was so attached to my baby cousin.

Even though many years had gone by, those ugly memories were still haunting me. There was a song that played regularly on the radio called Thanks for my Child by *Cheryl Pepsi Riley* that would always bring me to tears.

POISON RUNNING FREE

Technically, Evelyn was solely responsible for the baby, her first grandchild. She was the one who signed the discharge documents down in Maryland some several hours after the baby was born. I remember the night when the Jessup County Correctional Officer called us from the hospital to break the news.

"Hello? Grams said, answering the telephone.

"Yes, this is she....Great! That's wonderful news, 'cause we were worried about her ...Oh no no, we don't want that! We'll come and get her. I'm gonna have my daughter call you back and then you can give her the details as to where to come. Thank you so much for calling and letting us know."

Grams eagerly hung up the phone. She looked relieved, but at the same time disturbed.

"What happened Grams?" I asked.

"Renee' had the baby. She had a girl, but if a family member doesn't arrive at the hospital within 24 hours to get her, they'll put her up for adoption," she said as tears began to fall from her eyes.

Within hours, Evelyn, my mother and another cousin were in a rental headed for Maryland. The pressure was off. Well, to some extent at least. The biggest issue was who was gonna care for little Tameera while everyone else worked? The decision was unanimous: both families would care for her until her parents came home from prison.

On the weeks that she stayed with our side of family, I'd take her on the route with me. I always fixed her hair in the hottest styles, made sure she was well-kept, her clothes always being neatly pressed. In between the morning and

POISON RUNNING FREE

afternoon routes, I'd peel some potatoes, fry them up and douse them in ketchup. Then we'd eat, watch television and just chill together. I gave her healthy foods too, but french fries were absolutely her favorite. When it was time for her to go and be with Paul's family, it always killed me inside.

Those people were assholes. On two separate occasions, Tameera had been burned, or as they CLAIMED, had "accidentally" burned herself. The first time it happened, it was with the aunt's hot comb and on the second occasion, they claimed she had burned her face with that same aunt's curling iron. I didn't see how all this was possible, because Paul's sister never had any hair to begin with. I had nicknamed her"patchy scratchy" years ago. To me, the hair on her head resembled a mangy dog and she had the body of a cow. This girl had NO neck whatsoever with broad shoulders. She literally resembled a linebacker; and then had the NERVE to wear weaves. She must have

VENOMOUS MINDS 2

felt extremely uncomfortable when that glue bonded against her scalp.

During one of my afternoon routes, it was brought to my attention that Teddy had a girl riding with him in his van.

"Nishi, your boyfriend's cheatin' on you."

"What? Robert, shut up and sit your butt down," I told him.

"For real Nish. There's a girl in his van....look!" he said as he pointed towards Teddy's van. I seriously ignored this chatter box.

"Nishi, he's calling you now!" Robert shouted.

"Nishi look he's ..." This boy was getting on my last nerves.

"ROBERT! If you don't sit down and shut up, you'll be walking home! And when I pick you up in the morning,

POISON RUNNING FREE

just let me know what time you made it. Okay?" I sternly voiced. After that comment, I didn't hear another peep out of that brat.

Teddy WAS breaking his neck trying to get my attention though. Now he was holding his head out of his van window. *I gotta acknowledge this fool, `cause he knows that I see him* was my only thought.

"What is it?" I yelled to him. He frantically waved his hand, gesturing me to come in his direction.

"I can't! I have Tameera in the van with me," I shouted.

Actually, I could have gotten out if I'd really wanted to because Sandra was also with me that day. She was off on Fridays and had recently started riding with me during my afternoon route. I was hoping he'd leave well enough alone and go about his business; he slowly backed up alongside me.

"What's up?" he asked.

"Nothing."

"This is my sister." Ah shit, he's at it again. Could THIS be MooMoo?

"She just came the other day," he added.

"Hello," I said with a semi smile.

"Hello," the girl returned the greeting. Nahhh! This can't be MooMoo because this girl has no trace of testosterone in her voice.

"I'll see you later alright," Teddy said, pulling off so that his group could board his van. He pulled off without giving me a chance to answer. I wasn't trying to see him later, because it was Friday. Plus, it was family night.

"He's gonna come to your house tonight Nishi, so make sure you cook him some dinner and make sure that it tastes good! HA! HA!" This big mouth kid seriously

POISON RUNNING FREE

needed a muzzle. Robert was a pain in the ass, but he meant well.

Being around those kids every day, I grew very attached to many of them and, of course, Robert was one of them. There was this one little girl, Nikia - sweet and chubby. She was always into something, so I would give her candy and cookies on the slick side just so she'd be quiet. Then there was Mark - I adored him! Mark had asthma and I remember the day when his teacher hurried to the van as I pulled up.

"Nishi, I know that you have the other kids' to drop off, but I just want you to know that Mark is having an asthma attack," she explained. I looked down at him and saw that he was pulling for air.

"I called his mother and she said that his babysitter has his medicine there with her and will be waiting outside," the teacher continued on.

His teacher didn't have to say another word. I rerouted everything that day because I wasn't gonna have Mark collapsing on me. I sat him in the front passenger seat and consistently asked him if he was alright. Poor thing...all he could do was nod his head. It was killing me to see him in this condition.

As soon as I pulled up in front of the babysitter's house, she came running out with Mark's inhaler in hand.

"Wow you're early today!" she said while I helped Mark out through the driver door.

"Yeah because the teacher told me that he was having an attack, so I brought him straight in," I responded.

"He IS breathing kind of hard," the sitter recognized.

She shook the inhaler and placed it between his lips. Mark took two puffs as she knelt down in front of him.

"Can you breathe better now?" she asked.

POISON RUNNING FREE

"Yes!" Mark said.

PHEW! THANK GOD! I was relieved.

"I have asthma too and I know what it's like to be without air, which is why I never go anywhere without my inhaler," I explained to the sitter.

"I appreciate you going out of your way to bring him home first. I know his mother would say the same if she were here. She should be here soon because she left work early," the sitter explained.

While talking to the sitter the kids grew restless.

"HEY! HEY! STOP ROCKING THIS VAN!" I shouted at the fidgety group.

"Mark I hope you feel better, okay?" I rubbed his head.

"Okay," he softly responded while nodding his head.

VENOMOUS MINDS 2

That very same Christmas, Mark gave me a heart decorated mug. I barely used it and one day I realized that it was cracked from the rim down. I was so hurt, because this was the only thing that I had to remember him by. After that school year ended, I never saw him again, but he'll always have a place in my heart.

\*\*\*\*\*\*

Every Friday evening Evelyn and Ajaiwa were usually at the house between 6:30 and 7:00. It was customary for us to eat fast food, play cards and laugh all night. While Lee, Ajaiwa and Tameera played with one another, we'd partake in a game of Spades.

"What you waitin' for Gladys? Shuffle the cards!" Grams ordered after taking a sip of water. She was all geared up to play.

"Where's Evelyn?" she asked.

POISON RUNNING FREE

"I'm out here smokin' a cigarette!" Evelyn shouted from the backyard.

"Well come on because Gladys is dealing the cards!" Grams shouted back.

"Ms. Maron, you and Evelyn are partners right?" Sandra asked Grams while taking a seat across from my mother.

"Sandra you tryin' to start some shit right?" Grams snapped.

"Now Ms. Maron, WHY would I do that?" Sandra asked sarcastically as Evelyn took the only available seat, which just so happened to be directly across from Grams. "I'm just asking because you two always play the first game together."

Only a few hands into the game, the score was Sandra and my mother: 202; Grams' and Evelyn: 189.

"Evelyn, hold your hand up and stop showing Sandra all your damn cards!" Grams controlled her teammate.

"You two card sharks ready to bid?" my mother asked Grams and Evelyn.

"Evelyn, whatchu got?" Grams asked her partner.

"I think I can make three or four," Evelyn answered.

"Give us a nine!" Grams demanded.

Sandra and I began to laugh a little.

"Sandra what do you have?" my mother asked her partner.

"I got four....what about you?" Sandra said as she looked through her cards again.

"A possible two....we'll take five," my mother said filling in the score board as she threw down the first card. It was an Ace of Diamonds.

"Gladys, they're going in the hole with this hand," Sandra laughed. She was the family clown. In the beginning Grams didn't like her, but in time that all changed.

"No talking across the fuckin' board!" Grams said with a stern face as she played the Eight of Diamonds.

"Wait! Who threw down that Ace?" Sandra asked as she held her card in mid-air.

"Pay attention to the board!" Grams ordered. Sandra laughed and threw down the Seven of Diamonds.

"It's your turn Evelyn, whatchu waitin' for?" Grams stared at her partner.

VENOMOUS MINDS 2

"No talking across the board," Sandra repeated. Grams looked at Sandra and rolled her eyes. Evelyn threw out the Six of Diamonds. My mother gathered the cards to fold her first book.

After folding the book, she led with the King of Diamonds.

Grams cut her with the Ten of Spades. Sandra followed suit playing the Five of Diamonds and Evelyn, the Eight of Spades.

"Evelyn, you ain't got no more Diamonds...I hope you ain't just givin' cards away...and trumps at that?" Grams said, growing more and more uptight.

"Just play Grams," Evelyn responded.

Grams gathered the cards to fold the book then threw down the Ace of Hearts. Sandra cut Grams with the Seven of Spades.

POISON RUNNING FREE

"Shit! I should'a known that was gonna happen," Grams said, steadily growing more frustrated.

"Watch the board now! Play to win!" Grams stared at Evelyn.

"I thought it was no talking across the board," my mother reminded Grams. Evelyn played the Jack of Spades. My mother played the Five of Hearts. Grams collected the book.

"Go ahead Evelyn....play! You won that book." For a moment Evelyn paused, then played the Queen of Diamonds on the table. My mother suddenly snickered.

"Wait a minute! Y'all just reneged!" Sandra shouted, jumping out of her seat and frantically waving her hands.

"Well – ain't – THIS – some - shit! Evelyn didn't I ask you if you had any more Diamonds?" Grams was pissed!

"Just hand over your books – no sense complaining. Your partner messed up," my mother said, holding her hand out to collect the debt.

"Y'all in the hole already and it's only the beginning of the game …Hah–hah-haaa!" Sandra laughed loudly. Grams dropped the remainder of her cards on the table in disbelief.

BUZZZZZZ! The doorbell rang.

"I don't believe this shit!" I heard Grams say as I headed for the front door.

"It's probably your man Nishi!" Sandra projected her voice.

POISON RUNNING FREE

"What's up Nish?" The person at the door greeted me with a hug. I couldn't believe my eyes - it was Paul. Although our relationship had gotten off to a bad start, we'd somehow managed to set aside our differences.

"What's up? When did you get out?" I asked in amazement.

"Yesterday…well, really last night, 'cause by the time I got home it was late. Where's my daughter?" Paul spoke anxiously.

"Hold on... let me get her," I quickly returned to the kitchen area.

"Tameera, come here. Your daddy's here," I announced.

"What? Her daddy? Here?" I heard the card players say as they spoke among themselves in subtle tones. Everybody shuffled their chairs to clear a way for little

VENOMOUS MINDS 2

Tameera. Slowly, the little girl separated herself from her uncle and cousin, then ran to me.

"Come. Let's go see daddy!" I tried to lift her spirit.

"Daddy?" Tameera asked timidly. At the first sight of his baby girl, Paul immediately took her out of my arms.

"Hey Tameera Boo! How's daddy's big girl?" He kissed her several times, examining her face, both arms and then her legs. Evidently, he had heard about the burn stories too. Unenthusiastically, Tameera allowed this man, that she barely knew, to inspect her.

"So you got out yesterday huh?" I struck up a conversation.

"Uh huh," he replied.

"Did Renee' know that you were getting out?"

"Yeah," he answered.

I stood back so that he could become acquainted with his little girl.

"Paul what's up with the sneakers?" The don (Caribbean slang meaning – respected one) was wearing some white L.A. GEARS. It was clear that the sneakers weren't his because ONE, I could see that they were squeezing the shit out of his feet and TWO, they weren't Bally's.

"Oh these? These are my sister's sneakers. I'm about to go and do some clothes shopping now. Daddy's gonna come back for you later. Okay Meera boo?" Paul cooed at his daughter, handing Tameera back over to me.

"Okay," Tameera timidly replied.

"Nish, I just wanna do a little shopping and then I'll be back later to take her home with me," Paul explained.

VENOMOUS MINDS 2

"Alright," I replied. Before leaving, he leaned over and kissed Tameera one more time. She and I watched her daddy as he hobbled to his friend's car, which was extremely hilarious to watch.

\*\*\*\*\*\*

The most depressing part about this entire situation was that he and his brother were released from prison before Renee'. According to rumor, if Paul and his brother would've admitted the gun and drug paraphernalia were theirs, Renee' would not have done any time at all...or would have at least gotten out earlier; something like that. The unfortunate one still had several months left to go.

Upon returning to the kitchen, everyone had solemn looks on their faces.

"So that was Paul huh?" Grams smirked.

POISON RUNNING FREE

"Yeah, that black son of a bitch gets to come out while my daughter rots in that motherfuckin' cell...black bastard!" Evelyn expressed.

The card game didn't last much longer after Paul's unexpected visit, so instead of going the full distance, they ended the game at three hundred. Grams and Evelyn took blinds throughout the remainder of the game and unfortunately, they continued to drop further in the hole. By the end of the game, Grams was extremely unhappy.

"Just don't make no fuckin' sense!" Grams angrily voiced as she boxed up the cards.

BUZZ! BUZZ! Again, I went to answer the front door.

"Hey what's up?" This time it was Teddy standing there with an opened stout in his hand.

"I just saw Paul at dee' sto' (the store). I didn't know he was out," Teddy stated.

"Neither did we. It's a surprise to us too," I said, as the kids' entered the living room.

"HI TEDDY!" They all shouted at the top of their lungs.

"What's up kids?" Teddy returned their greeting and shook Lee's hand as if my baby brother were a big man.

"So what about Renee'? When is she coming out?" he asked as he took a seat on the couch.

"Well, the last time we visited her, she mentioned six months, and that was two months ago."

"That's fucked up muhn (man)." Teddy expressed.

"Yeah, it is, but hopefully it'll fly by fast 'cause I know she's feelin' it."

"Nish, I'm outtee five," Sandra said, breezing through the living room heading for the front door. The game was over, the mood had changed and there was no more loud laughter.

"What's up Teddy?" Sandra said in a low tone as she walked straight through without stopping.

"What up?" He replied, also in a low tone. I tried to make time for them both, my best friend and my lover, but the animosity between the two continued to grow.

"Nish …I'll talk to you later," Sandra shouted from the front door.

"Call me when you get home so I know you made it okay," I told her.

Of course she was fully aware of Teddy's living situation, and, I'm sure this was the reason she didn't care too much for him. Now Teddy's excuse for not liking

VENOMOUS MINDS 2

Sandra was that he felt she hung around me too much. I just hoped that one day they'd put their differences aside for the sake of me.

"You wanna go to the movies?" Teddy asked.

"When? Now?" I asked.

"Yeah! It's still early."

"Alright …let me go tell my mother I'm leaving…"

On the way back from the theater, something just didn't feel right. It seemed like the mood was off.

"Nishi, there's something that I have to tell you," Teddy hesitantly began.

"Yeah, what is it?" I asked, as I continued looking out the passenger window.

"Me dot'tuh's mudda (daughter's mother) is haye (here)."

POISON RUNNING FREE

"Your daughter's mother?" I gawked. "What daughter?"

"Me dot'tuh ...she lives in Grenada."

"Wait! So you have a daughter too?"

"Yeah."

"Well how old is she?"

"Six."

"WHAT! You have a big girl like THAT and you never even bothered to mention her to me?" I snapped.

"Nishi I didn't tell you all of this because I knew you would'a never talked to me."

"YOU DAMN RIGHT! So now it's TWO children by TWO different women?"

"Uh huh. And that's not all," he sighed. "Me first child's mother sent me a message saying that regardless of who I'm seeing, she wants me back."

At this point we were only about three or four blocks from my house.

"Oh yeah? Well you know what? YOU, your first baby's momma and MooMoo – y'all can have fun, because I want no part of this bullshit."

I jumped out of his van and slammed the door shut.

"Nishi, you didn't let me finish," he shouted through the passenger side window.

"Fuck off!" I yelled back and continued walking. This bastard must be crazy if he thinks I'm gonna put up with this shit. Every time I turn around it's some woman and another kid...

\*\*\*\*\*\*

POISON RUNNING FREE

For the next month or so, I ignored Teddy and his calls - AGAIN. Fortunately, I had something else to occupy my time.

"Nish, somebody told me that if we go out of state, the bikes would be cheaper," my mother randomly stated. Remember my mother's favorite phrase, "hook you up?" Well every so often, I'd remind her with the hope that she'd one day keep her promise. For years, I'd been doing her the favor of driving and it was now time for her to pay up.

"How far do we have to go?" I expressed my interest.

"Well, I called a couple of places and so far Pennsylvania has the cheapest prices."

"So when can we go?" I asked, as the adrenaline pumped throughout my body.

"If anything, probably after New Year's."

"Mommy! Next year?" I frowned.

"Yeah I know Nish, but I don't have four grand right now." She claimed after speaking with a salesman in Pennsylvania, the cost of a new bike ranged between four and six grand – depending on the make and model - of course. I really didn't care what type of bike it was, I just wanted a bike.

"Gladys I can lend you the money and you can just pay me back when you get it," Sandra stated while playing with Lee.

"Do you have it now?" my mother asked.

"No not on me, but it's at the house. Whenever you're ready to go, I'll just take the trip with y'all."

Man when Sandra said that I was happier than a pig in his slop!

POISON RUNNING FREE

"Okay. This will help me out and at the same time get Nish off my case. I'll call the guy tomorrow to get directions. You think we can go next weekend?" my mother asked Sandra.

"Yeah, like I said, whenever you're ready 'cause the money is just sitting there. I don't need it for anything right now," Sandra offered.

That following weekend we removed all but one seat from my mother's van and, along with Marvin, Sandra's older brother, we hit the road. Being that I didn't know too much about motorcycles, Marvin went with us to aid in my decision making. My choice really blew some minds but I remained humble, although, deep down inside, I knew I would be the talk of East Flatbush, Brooklyn. And, that's exactly what happened. People would refer to me as the girl with the red bike because they didn't know my name. I got the attention of many - children, adult men & women and even some police officers. This was because females weren't known to ride motorcycles back then. I rode a stock red Suzuki Katana 599 cc that many established bikers (which were men of various ages) use to call Katana's "can a tuna". I was not at all daunted by their lame joke(s) because I still earned my respect. Hatin' asses!

After weeks of having several lessons with Marvin, I was finally comfortable with doing upwards of 100mph with Sandra on the back. Usually after the rush hour when evening traffic died down, we'd head for the Belt Parkway and I'd open up that baby with my featherweight pillion.

Now this was the life! I often thought Sandra had a death wish; there is nothing in this world that would have gotten me on the back of someone's bike doing 100 mph – especially with a new rider that only possessed limited skills. I rode every day so those basic skills quickly improved, and now there was NO stopping me. On occasion, I'd ride my mother, but never at those speeds.

POISON RUNNING FREE

Now there was one time my mother and I went for a ride without our helmets – many people noticed us as our locks flapped in the wind. Each time we'd go for a ride, onlookers would admire us. People in the neighborhood thought we were sisters. My Jamaican neighbors across the street were my biggest fans. Every time I pulled in or out of my driveway, one of them would scream, "Bike riduh ...me beg yuh' for a ride!" I'd always wave my hand and tell them next time.

That summer flew by fast. I continued to ride in the fall and winter, which enabled me to brush up on my skills so by the time next spring rolled around, I'd be ready for the big boys. November was already here and to everyone's surprise Sandra and Rasta Rumps were kind of dating.

"Yo Nish, guess what? Rumps is supposed to be going to Teddy's house for Thanksgiving and he asked me to go with him," Sandra stated.

VENOMOUS MINDS 2

"For real?" I grew interested.

"Yeah."

"Well, are you going with him?" I asked.

"Nish, how would that look... me going to Teddy's house? I don't even like that tall skinny chump and he knows it. I barely even speak to him."

"So what? Just go so you can tell me how MooMoo looks."

"But what if she finds out that I'm your friend?"

"How? Who's gonna tell her? Teddy? Rumps? Come on Sandra, really?"

"Alright!" Sandra said emphatically. "I'll think about it. But IF I do, I'm not eating that chick's food. Bitch might put somethin' in it ...Ssssst!" Sandra sucked her teeth.

POISON RUNNING FREE

Ethon unexpectedly called my mother up one night asking for a visit. For years she hadn't heard from this guy. I believe he was just tired of the rough, dry touch of his cell mates' hands as they pried his buttocks apart, only to be smothered with some baby scented Vaseline as preparation for a stiff probe. He was now yearning for the soft touch of a woman.

Nah, he wasn't gay; well, not to my knowledge anyway. I DO know that he and his fellow inmates managed to see the Broadway play, *Dream Girls*. This play, and many others, were literally brought to them while they served their time in prison. This was made possible by the assistance of taxpayers and their generous "donations."

Unaware of what was discussed during that collect call, that very same weekend my mother packed some groceries and took the trip to see the menace of society. Grams and I were furious. What could possibly be the reason for her wanting to reconnect with this eyesore after all these years?

"Mommy, what are you doing?"

"Nishi, I know what you're thinking, but how much harm can he do me while he's in prison?"

"That's not the point!" I snapped at her. "Why even go see him? If you've moved on with your life, then a person like THAT shouldn't even be a part of it - especially, after what you've already been through!" I voiced.

"Please! It's just a visit," she huffed.

"Mommy ...he's never gonna change. Plus, now you have Lee to think about."

"One visit - THAT'S ALL." She spoke in a confident tone.

'If its closure that you want - I can give you closure...”

POISON RUNNING FREE

My mother was up to something. Ever since she'd gone to see Ethon, she seemed a bit on the reserved side.

"What's going on with you?" I asked her one day, a couple of weeks after the visit.

"I think that I may go again," she quietly replied.

"WHAT?! FOR WHAT?!" I shouted.

"Ethon mentioned to me that most of the visitors take either the train or a bus up there."

"So what does that have to do with you?" I didn't see the relevance. Being young can be a blessing and a course at times.

"Because Nish...if I get enough people to go Upstate with me, then I can make a nice set of money," she reasoned.

"I should have known it wasn't gonna be only one trip. He got you up there and told you this mess with the hope that you'd come back," I argued.

"But Nish, it makes sense though. With this extra money, I'll be able to pay off the van in no time. That's what I bought the van for right? To make money."

She DID make a valid point, but just the thought of her being involved with this creep again irked my nerves.

*******

One Saturday afternoon, about a week later, while I was in the shower, I heard someone knocked on the bathroom door.

"Yeah, who is it?" I yelled.

"Me!" the voice yelled back impatiently.

"Me who?" I shouted.

POISON RUNNING FREE

The individual then boldly opened the door. I slid the shower door back slightly to see the intruder.

"WHUT'S UP BIKE RIDUH?" The voice said loudly with a huge smile on her face. It was Renee! Just seeing her stand in that doorway brought so much joy to my heart, it was about to burst!

"Look at slim!" I smiled. "You lost a lot of weight! Hold up - let me get out!" I quickly grabbed my towel to dry myself off.

"Nah, don't rush 'cause I'm stop by again later."

"Where you goin'?" I asked.

"Gotta go see some of my friends. If they found out I was home and didn't let them know, they'll have something to say. I'll be back in an hour or so. Will you be here?"

"I should be. Sandra and I are going to see the movie *New Jack City* later, but I should be back by the time you return."

"How is Teddy?"

"He's alright. He asked about you too."

"Oh yeah? Tell him I said hi."

"Okay," I responded gleefully.

"Where's your black ass mother?" Renee asked, laughingly. Back in the day Renee would tease my mother about her dark complexion. Hence, she gave her the nickname "Black," and as time passed, I realized that my mother really had gotten much darker. It was later revealed to us that her drug use was likely the cause.

"She went to see Ethon."

"WHAT?! She's back with him?" Renee' frowned.

POISON RUNNING FREE

"Chile I don't know. She claims she can make a nice set of money if she carries passengers upstate to visit their incarcerated family members....hmm"

"Hmm....interesting! Oh well, let me go `cause I hear Paul blowin' the horn. See you later Nish," she said and quickly closed the door.

I was so happy to see her! She looked good; lost all of her baby weight and had snapped back to the old Renee'. I wish she could have stayed longer; then we could have caught up on old times.

Unfortunately, Paul was back to his old self. He was always trying to take control of my cousin, and for what? He was the snot rag that cheated on Renee' while she was still locked up. To my recollection, the chick that he cheated on her with was crazy desperate. This girl would just not let Paul and Renee' be at peace. Rumor had it, this same girl had gotten pregnant some time before Renee and Paul were locked up, but chose to abort the baby.

Later that evening, after returning from the movies, I was still all hyped about catching up on old times with my first cousin. Throughout our childhood years, many thought we were sisters and to date, they still do.

"Grams, did Renee' come back?" I asked.

"No she didn't, but she called to see if you were back from the movies and I told her no."

"Oh. Okay" I answered, a bit disappointed.

She didn't come back that day, but it was okay because at least my cousin was home again. Renee' had come home just in time for Thanksgiving and I know she was happy too; she loved Grams' sweet ma-tay-tuh pie (potato) as Grams would say. Grams would make about four to five pies and would give a whole one to Renee' to

POISON RUNNING FREE

take home. It was always a wonderful sight to see her in the kitchen preparing Thanksgiving dinner.

"Shit! Nish, do your grandmother a favor please?" Grams asked.

"What is it?"

"Run to the bank for me and deposit this money while I season this turkey. I meant to do it on my way home from work, but I forgot."

"Alright," I agreed. "Where's the money?"

"Hold on... let me get it." Grams washed her hands, grabbed her purse and pulled out the deposit envelope and her ATM card.

"You remember the code right?" she asked.

"Yes Grams. You send me to the bank almost every week. How can I not remember it?" I exited the house through the backyard door to where the van was parked.

VENOMOUS MINDS 2

"Nish, wait!" Grams hollered after me. "Here's twenty dollars. Pick me up a dozen of large eggs, two cans of cranberry sauce and some margarine too please."

"Is there anything else you want before I go to the bank and do some grocery shopping?" I asked, a hint of sarcasm in my tone.

"No that's it. Thank you darling," Grams smiled sweetly, acknowledging and ignoring my tone.

When I got back, I quickly dropped off her groceries then placed her ATM card and receipts in front of her on the kitchen counter.

"Grams, I'm going by Sandra's for a while. I'll be back in a few," I said and quickly headed for the front door.

*Let me get outta here before she remembers something else...*

\*\*\*\*\*\*

POISON RUNNING FREE

"Damn man! I had to park way down the block," I complained to Sandra as I rushed in from the cold. "It's too cold to be doin' all that walking!"

"Well shit is about to get real hot soon!" she exclaimed as we entered her room.

"Is your mother home?" I asked as I headed in behind her.

"Yeah, she's in her room watchin' football as usual."

"Oh okay. So are you going or what?" I took off my jacket, making myself comfortable.

"Yeah, I'm going. I told Rumps that I'm not eatin' anything though AND that when I'm ready to leave that's exactly what I mean."

"YES! This is going to be soooo funny-y-y. I can just imagine the look on Teddy's face when you walk through his door!" I giggled. "So what are you wearing?"

"Nish, you know I'm wearing some pants, `cause I might have to whip her ass in her own damn apartment if she finds out that I'm your best friend."

"Why do you say that? She's not gonna figure that part out."

"Nish c'mon….it's gonna be me, Rumps and I'm sure some of their other friends too. They know who the hell I am and they just might say something to her."

"Nah, I doubt it SO RELAX! I told Renee' that you might go and she said that we were crazy. I explained to her we had taken an oath and promised to be friends to the end."

POISON RUNNING FREE

"Yeah, that same damn oath might get my ass killed. Renee's right. I am crazy, `cause I don't believe I'm doing this shit myself," Sandra rolled her eyes.

"Stop stressin' girl! It's a date that you're going on and it just so happens that you and I know each other. Shit, it's a small world. Plus, Rumps is the one that asked you anyway; so, if any one catches the heat it's gonna be him. Now, as you say, I'm outtee! Call me when you get back and let me know how things went. What time are y'all supposed to be there?" I asked Sandra as I unlocked the top lock of her mother's apartment door.

"I told him I wanted to spend the majority of the day with my family, so we agreed that 7:30pm was a good time."

"So, you should be back around what? 9 or 10?"

"Hell NO! We're gonna be outta there within the hour!" Sandra snapped.

VENOMOUS MINDS 2

"You wanna hear a joke?" I asked Sandra.

"What joke? 'Cause right about now ain't shit funny," Sandra huffed.

"Be quiet and just listen. If she acts all shitty and stink with you, do like my mother and spit in one of her pots! HAAA!"

"Ahhh Nish, you're foul," she frowned.

"You know I'm just joking because that's some nasty shit. Anyway, let me go. Don't forget to call me tomorrow AS SOON AS YOU GET BACK!" I stressed.

"Believe me that's the first thing I'm gonna do after I take off my clothes."

"Later! And let's not forget - we're friends 'til the end," I reminded my good buddy.

"Get out of here, you fool!" Sandra said closing the door behind me.

POISON RUNNING FREE

The next morning, Grams got up to prepare the second half of her Thanksgiving dinner. Usually she'd do the majority of her cooking on the night before and would wake up around four o'clock a.m. on Thanksgiving Day to finish up.

"Gladys can you go pick up Mother and Daddy for me?" Grams asked, referring to her parents.

"Why can't Mother and Daddy take a cab? It's raining and I don't feel like going out," my mother rudely responded.

"Come on now," Grams begged her daughter.

"Come on now what? It would be so much easier if they would just jump in a cab and come over."

"Yeah, but the cab is so expensive. It costs me like nine - sometimes eleven dollars just to have them picked up," Grams explained.

VENOMOUS MINDS 2

"AND?" my insensitive mother responded.

"And what?" Grams looked puzzled.

"AND my van runs on gas too. You think it won't cost me to go way cross town and back?"

"Oh Lord! All of this I gotta go through just to get my parents over here for the day?" Grams complained.

"Every year you do this. Why can't somebody over THERE bring them over? All those people living in that house and NOBODY can bring them?" my mother argued back.

Regardless of how much Grams begged, my mother wasn't thinking of moving that van. Every year my great-grandparents spent Thanksgiving at our house, and my mother knew this, so I couldn't understand why she'd make such a big deal out of it THIS year.

"Nish, since your mother wants to act like an ASS, can you go get them for me?"

"Yeah, I'll go," I answered Grams.

"NO YOU'RE NOT!" my mother immediately shouted. "You are not moving that van!" My mother was seriously being an idiot.

"Gladys WHY NOT?" Grams frowned.

"Because I said so. I already told you that it costs me to run that van too."

"Fine Gladys! You want gas money?" Grams grew aggravated.

"Damn right! You'd have to pay the cab driver right?" My mother showed no remorse.

"If I give Nishi some gas money, can she pick them up?" Grams looked as if she was about to cry.

VENOMOUS MINDS 2

"As long as I have enough gas in my van for my Monday morning route..." She was being truly heartless.

I couldn't understand why my mother was being so cold hearted. These were HER grandparents we were talking about. They babysat Renee' and I from day one while they worked and/or partied until the wee hours of the morning. My mother must have been the richest, blackest, single female in Brooklyn. Was it possible that Grams cheated on my grandfather with Rabbi Rabinowitz and the end result was my mother, aka the black Jew?

The retrieval process was usually very slow because Ethlene and Livian moved like molasses. Poppa was what we called my great grandfather. He moved around a lot better than Granny though and I'm sure her excuses were her cumbersome "sisters" that had grown to resemble saddled bags that hung well pass her belly.

POISON RUNNING FREE

"Lee, make sure you hold me up while I step into the van," Granny told her husband while clutching her purse.

"Ahhh, just go on Ethuh. I got yuh," Poppa said.

"Lee hold me up now!" Granny grew nervous as she took her baby steps.

"I said just go on Ethuh!" Poppa grew somewhat annoyed.

He was a cool old man that didn't talk much, or should I say only spoke if there was any noise being made while his favorite television shows were on. Every day during the afternoon hours, he and Granny would watch Ironside and Hawaii Five-O. Now, if we made just a little noise, he'd threaten to use his strap, aka his belt, on us if "we didn't stop 'makin all that racket..."

Renee and I were only toddlers and just wanted to watch some cartoons. Usually after those boring shows went off, Poppa would give us his undivided attention.

"Y'all youngins wanna learn how to spell?"

"Yeah!" Renee and I would answer.

"Okay this is how you spell hippopotamus. H-I-P.. hip, P-O..po, P-O-T..pot, A-M-U-S.. hippopotamus!" He broke it down.

Although he'd threaten us on the regular, Poppa never hit us. He used to say that little girls were noisy, and one thing's for sure, he ALWAYS protected us. Each and every time our older boy cousins came downstairs to play with us, he'd chase them right out.

Having my great-grandparents over every Thanksgiving was a lot of fun.

POISON RUNNING FREE

"Nishi I thank you for pickin' us up," Granny said as she made herself comfortable in the front seat of van.

"You're welcome Granny," I responded.

"Whooo Wee! Look at this heap a rain fallin'. The weather man said that it was gonna rain, but I didn't think that it would be this much," Granny continued on.

"Yeah, it's a lot!" I agreed.

"I reckon Grams is finished with her cookin' huh?" Granny then asked.

"No not yet. I think she still has to bake the macaroni and cheese and her pies."

"Is Evelyn and her family there yet?" Granny continued on with her 21 questions, but I didn't mind.

"No not yet."

"What about Renee' and her little gal?"

VENOMOUS MINDS 2

"Nope. They'll probably get there just in time to eat."

"Haa – haa! Is that so?" Granny laughed.

As I pulled up in front of the house, Grams immediately ran out to the van.

"Hello! Hello! Happy Thanksgiving!" Grams greeted her parents.

"Hi there and Happy Thanksgiving to you too," Granny responded.

"Hello there! Happy Thanksgiving!" Poppa spoke.

"I didn't want y'all to get wet so I waited at the door with an umbrella. Boy - it sure took you long enough Nishi," Grams complained.

YOU UNAPPRECIATIVE...

POISON RUNNING FREE

I felt like asking her if she would've felt any better if I would've shoved her old ass parents into the van and tossed them around like a damn salad. But I didn't. I just let her talk.

"Come on Mother, you get out first," Grams instructed. "Daddy, you wait here until I get mother inside of the house and then I'll come back to get you."

"No that's okay, I ain't 'fraid no water. A little water ain't gonna kill me." Poppa mumbled as he shifted himself to get out. Grams and I looked at one another and laughed. Poppa was a very stubborn and strong old man. He was also a very heavy drinker, but gave it up after experiencing many embarrassing urinating episodes and dangerous falls which resulted in him getting concussions.

"Happy Thanksgiving Granny!" My mother greeted her grandmother as she entered the kitchen.

"Thank you. Thank you. Same to you," Granny replied.

"How's everything?" My mother had now made her way over to Granny and gave her a kiss on the cheek. Really?

"Oh I'm doing okay. Well at least, that's what the doctor say. My back was hurtin' me a little, so he gimme some pain killers to take, but I reckon they ain't too good 'cause my back still aching me. He told me to take two pills a day, but I take fo (four) or five of 'em sometimes," Granny explained.

"MOTHER, YOU TAKIN' TOO MUCH!" Grams raised her voice.

"Yeah, but if I don't take 'em, I still feel a li'l pain," Granny added.

POISON RUNNING FREE

"Lord Mother, you gonna kill yourself by taking so much pain killers!"

"Hey Poppa! You lookin' sharp as ever! Let me take your coat and hat," my mother greeted her grandfather. Really? I mean Really?!

She was so full of shit. Little did my great-grandparents know this same fool didn't even want to pick them up in the van that was leased in Gram's name.

"Gimme a glass! You gotta glass?" Granny asked after taking a seat at the kitchen table.

"What you want Mother? What you need a glass for?" Grams asked her mother.

"I wanna put my teeth in it. I need to rinse 'em off so I can eat my food later."

"Oh Ethuh, I don't know why you couldn't do that at home," Poppa voiced.

"You got some Alka Seltzer? I got a li'l gas in my chest."

"Mother what did you eat to get the gas?" Grams questioned her mother.

"I had a chicken sammich from around the corner and I reckon it must'a been too greasy."

"Now Mother, you know you ain't had no business eatin' nuttin' from around nobody's corner. You know `dem people nasty as hell 'round dere and they probably fried it in lard too," Grams chastised her mother.

Now just listen to these country ass folk. We had Nachez, Mississippi right there in our very own kitchen.

"Mother, I got some ginger ale. You want that instead?" Grams asked.

POISON RUNNING FREE

"Yeah, gimme that and put'ta li'l ice in it for me too," Granny requested. Grams filled the glass half way and handed it to her mother.

"Where `da ice at?" Granny frowned.

"Lord Mother, you don't need no ice!"

"Don't tell me what I don't need," Granny said, eyeballing her daughter. "I SAID gimme some ice." Grams huffily about-faced, walked over to the refrigerator, reached into the ice maker, grabbed two cubes, returned to the kitchen table and dropped them in Granny's glass.

"You sure stingy wit duh ice," Granny stated with an attitude. We all laughed out loud.

******

By 4:00 the entire family was present. Grams had finished cooking and it was time for us to eat. Every year Poppa said grace and every year his prayer was consistent

VENOMOUS MINDS 2

with last year's prayer and the year before that and the year before that. We all gathered around the dining room table and bowed our heads.

*"Heavenly father, we thank you for this meal that you have placed before us and thank you for the cook. Lord, we thank you for giving us another year to enjoy and to be with our family on this day. Lord, we thank you for our health and we look forward to many more Thanksgivings. Amen!"*

"Amen!" the family concurred.

Usually the kids and the men ate first.

"Daddy, I'm gonna put a little bit of everything on your plate okay."

"It don't matter to me, just as long as you have 'dem black-eyed peas on it," Poppa answered.

POISON RUNNING FREE

"Lee, come boo. Tell me what you want," my mother called out to my little brother.

"Tameera!" Renee' shouted. This went on until all the kids were eating and then the women would prepare their plates.

As Grams began to enjoy her meal, she realized Evelyn wasn't eating.

"Evelyn aren't you gonna make yourself a plate?" Grams asked.

"I'm just waitin' for the kids to finish eatin', 'cause whatever they don't eat, I will." Evelyn explained.

Evelyn was our human garbage disposal. She would devour the kids' leftovers, in addition to her own personal plate. She was a stern believer in recycling.

"Renee' hand me my teeth! I need my teeth," Granny ordered.

"Huh?" Renee' frowned. She had no idea as to what our great-grandmother was talking about.

"Never mind, I'll get 'em, 'cause Renee' don't know what you talking about Mother," Grams said as she placed her fork on her plate and slid her chair from beneath her.

"Dese greens a li'l too tough for me and I need muh teeth to chew 'em," Granny explained to us. By then Grams had returned with the glass. Renee' looked at me and hysterically began to laugh.

"What's wrong with you fool?" I mumbled under my breath while laughing with her.

"Nishi, why is her teeth in a drinking glass?" Renee' lowered her head and asked in a low tone.

"Girl, before y'all got here, she asked Grams for a glass so she could rinse off her teeth," I explained.

"You gotta be kiddin' me," Renee' laughed.

POISON RUNNING FREE

"Nope. You see her teeth in the glass right?"

"Remind me to bring my own glasses with me when I come over here from now on," Renee' added.

"You're stupid," I said and laughed.

"No I'm not. I'm serious, 'cause that's some nasty shit."

Around 8:00, everyone was full and just about ready to leave. Being that Poppa and Granny were going Evelyn's way, she took them home, along with this huge bag of food for Wasobi. The medical student stayed home that year to study for his upcoming exams. Honestly, I really don't think he cared at all about missing this event, because he wasn't too fond of my mother. My uncle had once mentioned to Evelyn that he didn't like his sister-in law, because there was something extremely evil about her. He never said exactly what it was, but he reminded Evelyn to steer clear of her deceitful sister.

**VENOMOUS MINDS 2**

"Let me scald this glass out that Mother had her teeth in," Grams said as we cleared the dining room table. She clenched Granny's temporary teeth rinser and headed for the kitchen.

"Please. You need to throw that glass out," Renee' suggested.

"Haaa! Stop it Renee'. It will be alright once I scald it out," Grams laughed.

"Uhhp! There's Paul. I hear him blowing. Tameera, tell Lee you'll play with him later 'cause daddy's here. Hurry up - we gotta go!" Renee' grabbed her belongings and rushed to put on their coats. Again Renee' was jumping for Paul.

Periodically, she'd come over to relax with us and he made sure the duration of her visit was short because within the hour, he'd return and blow the shit out of his car horn. I couldn't understand why she let this fool run her like

POISON RUNNING FREE

this. He had already stopped her girlfriends from calling and coming over. Every time he blew that horn, I felt like running out there to ask him if he had a freakin' problem and why was he keeping tabs on my cousin like that. But who was I to talk? Look at my situation.

I'm sure people, other than Sandra, wondered why I continued to date Teddy, and to be honest with you, I couldn't figure that out myself, but one day Evelyn helped me sum it up.

She expressed it was a pattern I obviously wanted to break. Being that I wasn't raised by my father, I desired the love of a man, even if it wasn't under the best circumstances. Teddy resembled my father a lot, which made the situation even more confusing. I wanted him around, but at the same time I didn't because of what he really was – a male whore. When Evelyn revealed this fact to me, it didn't make much sense, but in time the mystery would be solved.

VENOMOUS MINDS 2

At approximately 9:30 p.m. that night, the phone rang.

"Hello," I answered.

"Girl you know you are so right about Meryl. She IS a MooMoo!" Sandra stated loudly.

"For real! How does she look?" I asked eagerly.

"She's about my height, a little bigger than me though, and she's real dark."

"What did Teddy say when he saw you walk in?" I asked impatiently.

"He's the one that opened the door for us. You could see that he was surprised, but he just played it off," Sandra answered.

"So did she say anything to you?"

"No, but her sister offered me a plate of food and I said, 'no thank you.' Rumps didn't eat anything either; he just had a beer. MooMoo sat up under Teddy all night like she was SO IN LOVE and every time he moved, she followed him like a puppy..."

"...On one occasion, he got up and sat on the other end of the couch when she went into the kitchen to do something; I don't know what she did, but when she came out, she walked right over to Teddy and sat in his lap. You could tell he was uncomfortable because any other man would have hugged his girl or showed some type of affection, but he just sat there looking stupid. He barely talked. She did all the talking - she and her sister. They look like they run shit up in that apartment..."

My friend 'til the end' gave me ALL the details.

"Was any of his family there?" I asked.

"Nope... just her sister and his friends."

VENOMOUS MINDS 2

"Did you see the baby?"

"Yeah he was there. He's tall for a three year old and hairy just like his punk ass daddy. He's a cute little boy though. He don't look nothing like MooMoo, with her hanging bottom lip. You should'a seen her hair. She didn't even bother to comb it. I can see why he gave you his number... his girl at home looks like shit."

"Oh well. I'm sure he's gonna say something to me about this unexpected visit, but WHATEVER - fuck him!" I voiced carelessly.

"For real, `cause he aint nothin' but a lying bastard anyway. Yo, I'm gonna jump in the shower and go to bed, `cause I gotta be to work tomorrow at 8 in the morning."

"Thanks for going, shorty," I expressed appreciatively.

POISON RUNNING FREE

"Oh, no doubt - no doubt. Remember....friends to the end. If I don't see you during the week, I'll be over there Friday to do the route with you in the afternoon," she informed me.

"Alright, go and get some sleep. I'll talk to you later."

"Later," Sandra said, hanging up the phone.

*"TEARS"*

*TEARS OF HAPPINESS*

*TEARS OF SADNESS*

*TEARS HAVE MANY MEANINGS*

*ALL TEARS THEY HAVE THEIR OWN STORIES*

*IT CAN TELL US OF HURT*

*LOVE*

*OR GREAT GLORY!*

Usually, everyone has the day after Thanksgiving off to relax and eat left overs, but not my mother. She was making calls to her regulars trying to arrange a trip upstate. Fortunately, only two returned her call, but the two wasn't enough for her to make the trip.

POISON RUNNING FREE

"Hopefully next weekend I'll get a nice crowd. Everybody's probably broke after the holiday weekend," she reasoned.

Unfortunately, this trip thing went on for a while. Was she making any real money? NO, but that didn't matter because, once again, she was in touch with her old flame. What was the attraction? And rumor had it that he was now married to his child's mother, which was their get high (crack) partner back in the day. So yeah, this was one big happy family.

Several weeks had gone by and Gladys was still slippin' and slidin' on those bumpy, hilly and winding roads of Ossining, New York.

"Hey Ree, what's up?" I answered the phone on this particular night.

"Nishi," Renee said, sounding very upset. "I just found out that the bitch was pregnant again with Paul's baby while I was locked up."

"Renee' you been cryin'?" I asked.

"No."

"Yes you was`cause I can hear it in your voice. Is he there now?"

"No. He left when I confronted him about it," she whimpered, blowing her nose.

"How did you find out?" I asked her.

"'Cause two of my friends told me. That's why he didn't want me to see or talk to any of my friends; he knew they would tell me about that bitch gettin pregnant again."

"Do you want me to come over there?" I asked.

"No, because he's coming back soon."

POISON RUNNING FREE

"How do you know?"

"Because he didn't drive. I think he went across the street to his mother. If Tameera wasn't sleepin' I would have asked you to come and pick us up."

"You need to stop cryin', 'cause it's pissing me off. Remember, you are the one who told me that men always lie and how I shouldn't let them fuck my head up. The same applies to you," I reminded her.

"But Nishi that's only the half of it." CO-N-N-N-K! She blew her nose again.

"What do you mean half of it?" I asked.

"I'm pregnant again," Renee' whispered.

"What?!" I screamed into the phone. "Are you serious?"

"Yes," she sniffed. "I was supposed to have gotten my period last week, but it never came."

VENOMOUS MINDS 2

"Does he know?" I asked, pretty much knowing what the answer would be.

"Yeah, because that's how the whole argument started."

"Well I know you're keeping it - right?"

"Nishi what am I gonna do with two kids? I'm only twenty years old."

"If you can make it with one, you'll make it with two." Listen to me, giving THAT kind of advice!

"But I just got out of prison. Who's gonna hire me with a felony?" Damn, this bastard was a real fuck up. He had totally screwed her life up.

"Ree, don't worry about it. It'll be alright."

"What do you mean don't worry about it?!" She wailed. "I gotta worry! How am I gonna feed two kids with

POISON RUNNING FREE

no job? Because THIS selfish bastard SURE as hell can't do it! All he knows how to do is hustle..."

"The only thing I can say is that you'll make it. It might ....."

Suddenly Renee interrupted me.

"Nish I gotta go, 'cause I hear his keys in the door," Renee' spoke in a very low tone. She seemed terrified.

"I'll pass by you tomorrow morning after the route okay?" I told her.

"Okay – bye!" She whispered and quickly hung up the phone.

The next morning, I saved my mother some gas and rode my motorcycle over to Renee's. By the time I got there, everything between her and Paul had been squashed. She told me that one of her friends had told her how to get medical coverage for herself, Tameera and the unborn child.

VENOMOUS MINDS 2

"Nish. I'm gonna call you later and let you know how things went." Being that things were calm, there was no need for me to stay, so I left.

As soon as I returned home, the phone rang.

"Hello?" I answered.

"Hi. Good morning. How was you (your) T'anksgiving (Thanksgiving)?"

It was Teddy.

"It was fine and yours?" I coolly responded.

"You know 'cause you friend told you already," he said, his tone dripping with sarcasm.

"Whatever! I hope you didn't call me to get on my nerves this morning," I snapped back.

"No I didn't, but I want you to do me a favor."

"Why don't you ask your daughter's mother to do you the favor since she wants you back," I snapped again.

"That's what I want to talk to you about, but you never answered me calls."

"Why should I? So you can fuckin' tell me some bullshit lie? You got a problem!"

"Yeah, me problem is you."

"Excuse YOU you lying ass bitch!"

"You heard me....me problem is you! I don't know what you did to me, but I can't get over you!"

"Well you need to try harder!" I told him.

Although he heard me say try harder, deep down inside I meant 'I can't get over you either.' I was so in love with this fool it wasn't even funny.

**VENOMOUS MINDS 2**

"So can you do me dee favor?" Teddy asked me again.

"What is it?"

"I have to watch me son this morning, but he's sick and I want some bread from dee bakery."

"So what does that have to do with me?"

"I want you to go get it and bring it to me."

"What? You must be crazy. Where's MooMoo?"

"She not haye (here)."

"But what if she comes and sees me there?" I asked.

"She won't because she is way in Manhattan."

This is crazy. First Sandra and now *he's* trying to get me over there. How disrespectful of him to invite me over to this woman's dwellings!

"So are you going for me?" He spoke with authority.

POISON RUNNING FREE

"Which bakery?" I asked.

"Dee one on Utica near Carroll Street. And when you get haye, ring bell 3C and I'll buzz you in."

"I'm tellin' you now, if she comes home and gets in my face - it won't be nice..."

It didn't take long to complete the trip to the bakery and head over to his apartment because the two were literally only blocks apart. When he opened the door, I saw that he was wearing shorts and the little boy was holding onto his pale leg for dear life.

"Come in," he said. I handed him the bread and remained by the door.

"You scared?" he asked me. I looked at him as if he were a jackass that had lost his mind.

"No, but I'm not about to have some bitch run up on me either," I voiced quietly.

VENOMOUS MINDS 2

"Have a seat!" The little boy was watching me like a hawk. *Baby, I know I look better than your mother but she can't help her ugliness.* Slowly the little one approached me and motioned for me to pick him up.

"Pick he up!" Teddy insisted.

"Are you crazy? If Meryl found out that I held her baby, she would probably wash him in ammonia."

The kid was still reaching for me, but I just couldn't.

"Don't be so stupid, gyul," Teddy said.

"Nah, that's alright. You pick him up. He's YOUR son."

"Yeah, but he not richin' (reaching) for me though."

"Well," I shrugged, turning away. I focused my attention on a picture album lying on their coffee table.

POISON RUNNING FREE

"Can I look at these pictures over here?" I asked, finally, slowly entering the apartment.

"Go ahead," he walked into the kitchen with the bread in his hand.

"Is this MooMoo?"

"Waye (Where)?" he said, coming out of the kitchen while holding a knife.

"Right here," I pointed to the picture of a young woman.

"Yeah, dat's she."

"Figures. And who is this standing next to her?"

"Dat's she mudda and she sister from last year's T'anksgiving."

"And who are these girls over here?" There was a whole gang of them.

VENOMOUS MINDS 2

"Dat's she udder (other) sisters'."

"Damn. How many sisters' does she have?"

"It's fo (four) of dem."

"Is Moo Moo the oldest?"

"No."

Well she looks like it from these pictures," I laughed.

He sucked his teeth and removed the album from my hands.

"Whatever – I've had enough of looking at the gruesome Grenadian sisters' anyway. She said that if she ever saw you she's gonna kill you," the male whore relayed the crazy message with this idiotic smile on his face.

"Excuse me? I will tear MooMoo up," I assured him.

"I don't know about that. She strong muhn (man)."

POISON RUNNING FREE

"Maybe to you, but look at you. You're 6'2" and you weigh no more than 120 lbs, so anybody's strong compared to you."

"You ahss (ass)," he snapped back.

"No more than you. You are the idiot that invited me up here. Can I see the rest of the apartment?" I asked, but had already begun to stroll through their place.

"Yeah, why not?" He replied with just a hint of sarcasm. He seemed to have no objections to my request and seemed very relaxed. The kitchen was small and so was the bathroom.

"OH NO! I know that ain't her big ass bloomers hanging over the shower curtain," I shouted in disgust. MooMoo had about three pairs of bloomers dangling from the curtain rod. Must be her period panties.

"Go on gyul!" He gently pushed me along.

VENOMOUS MINDS 2

"Is this your room?" I asked.

"Yeah."

"Your son sleeps in here with y'all too?" I asked questions as I walked through the apartment.

"Yeah - what's wrong with that?"

"Don't you think that he should have his own room? 'Cause you three are packed in here like sardines and what ...?" I caught myself.

"And what? What if we have sex? We don't. I haven't had sex with this gyul for weeks now. She said that she's scared that she'll get pregnant again," he explained with a straight face.

"You sound like a fool. Do you really expect for me to believe that dumb shit?"

"You wanna give me some right now?" Teddy boldly asked.

POISON RUNNING FREE

"You gotta be crazy. You are so disrespectful. It's bad enough that I'm up here – and what is that?"

I pointed to a round rubber looking cover with ribbed edges.

"What?" He turned and looked in that direction.

"Is that a diaphragm?"

"Gyul, it's time for you to go. You too dahm (damn) nosey."

"Wait!" I shrugged my shoulders, getting out of his grip.

"That IS a diaphragm! What a nasty bitch! She just lays it around like that What if the baby gets a hold of it and puts it in his mouth? Yuk."

Just the thought disgusted me.

VENOMOUS MINDS 2

"Let's go! It's time for you to leave," he redirected me to the living room.

"With your lying ass ...I thought you hadn't had sex with her in weeks."

"Bye Nishi."

"Bye – liar!" I went through the door.

Now that I knew how she looked, I scanned the block to see if she was nearby.

Renee' called me after the evening route that day.

"Nishi, I just called to let you know everything went well today. I found this clinic that accepts Medicaid, which covers the prenatal visits and everything else right up until the baby leaves the hospital," she explained in a relaxed tone.

"Good! You see? I told you it was gonna work out. You were working yourself all up for nothing."

POISON RUNNING FREE

"Still Nishi....TWO kids?" she sighed. "But anyway girl," she said, changing the subject, "let me tell you what YOUR mother did."

"My mother?" I asked with surprise.

"Yep. That black ass Gladys. While I was locked up, my mother mentioned to me that your mother had asked her if she could claim Tameera on her taxes - right?"

"Uh huh," I nodded.

"Well my mother told her no, because she was already claiming Tameera due to the fact that she was the legal guardian since birth."

"Uh huh. Go on." I so wanted her to get to the point.

"Well my mother just received a letter from the I.R.S stating that someone else was using Tameera's social security number along with her."

"GIRL...YOU'RE LYING!" My eyes widened.

VENOMOUS MINDS 2

"No I'm not – and my mother is FURIOUS. But they told her not to worry, because as long as she can prove she was the legal guardian for the years that I was away, then she'll be o.k. Now as for your mother, she's going to be audited. Girl - I don't know what's wrong with her. And to think, we're just NOW finding this out all because I'm applying for these medical benefits."

Apparently, the grand larceny charges that led to my mother's arrest many years ago didn't faze her; appeared she was at it again.

"That's a federal crime you know," Renee' added.

"I know," I agreed.

"I don't know about your mother. She got issues - that shit was dead wrong. My mother told her NO and yet she STILL did it. That's the part I can't understand," Renee stressed.

POISON RUNNING FREE

"Oh please. That ain't even as half as bad as what she asked me to do."

I began to reveal my story.

"If it has something to do with your mother - I can only imagine."

"My mother is married you know!"

"WHAT? TO WHO AND WHEN DID THIS HAPPEN?" Renee's bellowed.

"She said that he's African. According to the story she gave me, or should I say us, because Sandra was there with me, she said this guy paid her FIVE THOUSAND DOLLARS to marry him."

"WHAT THE...!" Renee blurted.

"Hold on – wait a minute!" I said, setting Renee up for the kill. "She said that when he gets his papers, he'll pay her the remaining five."

VENOMOUS MINDS 2

"You gotta be kiddin' me?"

"Nope! But Ree, the thing is, she asked me and Sandra to do it too."

"ARE YOU SERIOUS?" Renee yelled again.

"Yep, she's a trip. She made it seem like doing this was nothin'. These were her exact words,

*'It's an easy $10,000 for y'all to make and after the guy gets his papers y'all can get a divorce. Y'all are still young and it ain't like y'all are gonna get married to a REAL boyfriend any time soon anyway so, why not do it? I hear that they like younger girls too – he asked me if I had any friends that might be interested in makin' some money & I told him that I would ask around...'*

Ree, your aunt has ISSUES! "

POISON RUNNING FREE

"Yeah I can see that," she responded and released a long sigh.

"Well, when do you go to the doctor?" I asked, needing to change the subject.

"My first visit is next week, and I can already see this pregnancy is gonna be so different compared to my first one..." She still sounded somewhat worried.

"Why do you say that?"

"Because last time I was in prison and didn't even know when I was in labor. I was getting all these cramps and didn't know why. Then like about 4:00 in the morning I woke up because my bed was wet. I thought I had peed myself, so I called the guard and asked her for some clean sheets. She asked me why and I explained to her that mine were wet. She was the one who realized that my water had broke and called the paramedics, but by the time we had arrived at the hospital, the doctors said that most of my water had seeped out and I was having a dry birth," Renee explained.

"What's that?" I asked.

"The doctor's explained to me that the amniotic sac had very little fluid and I'd feel more pain when pushing. The fluid helps the baby slide easier through the canal."

"Did it hurt?" I asked. The topic interested me.

"HELL YEAH THAT SHIT HURT! But it didn't hurt as much as when they told me my baby was going to be put up for adoption if someone didn't pick her up within twenty four hours. Nish, I cried like a baby."

That was the first time Renee' had ever spoken to me of her experience in prison. I guess she had to settle in and find her comfort zone once again in the real world before she could elaborate on her unfortunate encounter with the judicial system.

POISON RUNNING FREE

BEEP

"Hold on Ree – somebody's on the next line."

"Nah go ahead. I'll talk to you later," she said.

"Okay."

The phone beeped a second time. I quickly clicked over.

"Hello."

"Haylo is this Nishi?" I knew who it was from the moment she said hello.

"What are you calling here for?" I asked.

"I just wanna let you know that you can have Teddy. Earlier I asked him if he loved you and he said yes, so I told him to go to his slut which is you and the only reason why you can have him now is because I give him to you. So remember that," she blurted.

**VENOMOUS MINDS 2**

"Your momma's a fucking slut," I voiced loudly.

BLAM! The bitch slammed her phone down. This was the same shit that my mother and Grams would go through with other women. Was history repeating itself?

RING! RING! The phone rang again.

"Tell Teddy that his clothes are..." Meryl started out, but I quickly interrupted.

"BITCH - tell him yourself and maybe he'll tell you that he loves me again!"

I controlled the conversation. BLAM! She hung up again.

RING! I answered it again, but this time I spoke first.

"I can't help it if you don't know how to keep your man," I quickly stated.

POISON RUNNING FREE

"SLUT!" MooMoo quickly shouted and hung up.

This situation was totally crazy, but I had to call her back.

"I already told you MooMoo - I didn't approach him. He approached me."

"Yeah. But you are the slut that slept with him. I hope you two have a happy life together."

This bitch was getting on my last nerves with this "slut" shit, so I grabbed those van keys and just as I was about to drive it out of the garage, Teddy walked up.

"Why is your bitch calling me? I stopped calling your house when I found out that she was your girlfriend AND your child's mother, so what's her fuckin' problem now?"

"I told she that I didn't love she, so she got upset and threatened to kill you."

VENOMOUS MINDS 2

"Haaa!" I laughed.

"I knew she was gonna call you because she kept saying that she was."

"And for what?" I asked.

"That's what I said too, but dis gyul is stchewpid (stupid). When she gets mad, she says and does stchewpid things."

"So why did you tell her that you loved me if you knew that she was going to act stupid?"

"Because I'm tired of she and she shit. It was time for she to know dee trute (the truth.)."

Instantly, our eyes locked. This was the first time in his life he had PROBABLY spoken truthfully.

"LOVE? That's funny. If you love me then why did you feel the need to tell her everything about us?" I questioned him.

POISON RUNNING FREE

"Nishi 'cause I didn't know that I was gonna fall in love wid you. It just happen muhn. I told you that already and plus, she's mad about sometin (something) else too."

"What?"

"One night when me and she were havun' sex, I called out you name."

"Such an ass!" I laughed at his statement, actually beaming on the inside.

"That happened after me and you had come back from Florida, but I never told you."

"Teddy. All I have to say is that...." I paused.

"What?" He asked.

"You can't stay here! My grandmother's not havin' it!"

"I know that. I gotta find me a place. She sister stays there sometime too and I'm tired of 'dee whole ting (thing)."

He dug in his pocket and pulled out his pack of Newports.

"Where were you going?" he asked while lighting the cigarette.

"Nowhere," I lied. "Where's your van?" I turned and asked him.

"I walked haye (here)."

"WALKED?" I frowned.

"Yeah because I didn't want to lose my pack."

"Your pack?" I asked.

"My pack! My pack! My spot gyul," he kept saying.

"Oh-h! Your PARK. Learn how to open your mouth and speak man," I said.

POISON RUNNING FREE

"You should talk gyul. You should learn how to keep you eyes clean because every time I turn around you have boo boo in dem. I'm gonna start calling you dee boo boo factory."

Not only was Teddy a whore, but he was also full of sarcasm.

"Fuck you ass-face!" I replied.

"Yeah, you can dish it, but you can't take it. I know you type. You have some in you eye right now," he said as he looked closer. "Shi-i-i-i-t muhn! In bote 'a dem'." (both of them) he added.

Too embarrassed, I quickly turned away from him to remove the cold from my eyes. We talked for a while longer and later I drove him home.

"Alright Mr. Ted, you're home!" I parked on the opposite side of his building and leaned over to kiss him goodbye. Upon opening my eyes at the end of our kiss, I saw someone approaching the van from a distance in the passenger side view mirror.

"Teddy is that MooMoo?" I pulled away from him.

"Whaye (Where)?"

"Look in the mirror." Just as he looked in the passenger side view mirror, the person started to run towards my mother's van.

"Drive gyul!" Teddy unexpectedly yelled.

"Is that her?"

"Yes it's she. Just drive!" He waved his hand, gesturing me to pull off.

"For what? I aint scared of her."

"Nishi just drive please!"

POISON RUNNING FREE

I calmly switched the gear into drive. As I slowly pulled off I realized that MooMoo was holding a broom, trying to run down the van.

"Shi-i-i-t muhn! Why dee fuck don't she leave me alone?"

I couldn't believe this crazy bitch. Since she was acting like a mental patient, I had to mess with her a little. I slowed down just a bit, so she could catch up to us and just when she got closer, I hit the gas. I know this maniac didn't really think that she could run down and CATCH an eight cylinder van. But then again, crazy people don't think....they just act.

"Nishi stop playin' and just drive `dee van," he begged.

"Who's upstairs with your son while she's down here acting like a damn fool?" I asked.

VENOMOUS MINDS 2

"Nobody," he responded. "She sister isn't daye (there).

This girl's an idiot.

This went on for several minutes until I decided to go and park somewhere else.

"Look....it's getting late and I have to get up early in the morning to do the route, so if you wanna stay out here and run from your mad woman all night, that's fine with me, but I gotta go," I told him.

He looked at me with this fearful look in his eyes. I felt sorry for him, but what could I do? What HE needed to do is let her know who the MAN is and stop running like a damn punk.

I arrived home at 1:30 that morning. Crazy ass chasing the van. I should'a let her catch up to it to see if she was really all that bad. HUH! HUH! I laughed out loud

POISON RUNNING FREE

while pouring myself a glass of orange juice before going to bed.

As I reached the top of the staircase, Grams exited the bathroom.

"Somebody called here about an hour ago looking for you," Grams stated as she slowly walked back towards her bedroom. "She said that she was Teddy's old lady."

She apparently had been awakened from the early morning call and found it hard to fall back to sleep. That bitch! What the hell is she calling here so early in the morning for with that dumb shit? It's on now! Grams had no idea that Teddy lived with a woman, but she did now.

"Fuck her and him too!" I mumbled to myself.

Without even thinking, I headed back to his place. I arrived within minutes and double-parked alongside his van. I seriously hoped that he'd be in it and saw me, but he had

VENOMOUS MINDS 2

gone in; his absence made me angrier and I began to talk to myself.

"Motherfucker - I'm so tired of you and your bitch. This shit is gonna end right now and I don't give a fuck."

I grabbed the screwdriver from beneath the front passenger seat of my mother's van, jumped out and calmly scratched the driver's side of his van from front to back. To make matters worse, I added a few drops of crazy glue to his van door locks.

"This should teach him – wanna lie and fuck with my head?" I muttered to myself. I even applied a few drops of glue to the newly deepened scratches.

Around 9:30 a.m. that same morning, he called, questioning me like the fool that he was.

"Nishi, did you scratch me vahn (van) up last night?"

POISON RUNNING FREE

"Last night? How could I scratch your van up when I was with you the whole freakin' night?"

"Well somebody scratched it up and they put some kind of glue on two of me locks."

"Are you serious?" I asked calmly, but deep down inside I was laughing my ass off.

"When I went to warm up me vahn this morning I couldn't poosh (push) my key in and dee glue is on the body of dee vahn too. From the locks it dripped down onto dee doe (door)," he explained.

"Probably was your MooMoo," I said.

"No. It wasn't she." He sounded sure.

"Oh? And how do you know this?"

"Because I asked she and she said it wasn't she."

VENOMOUS MINDS 2

"From the way that she was acting last night – you believe her?"

"Yeah, I don't tink (think) she'd lie like that."

"You'd be surprised as to how much you don't know a person. Just like how I didn't and STILL don't know YOUR ass," I snapped.

"What are you doing now?" he asked.

"Nothing I just got in about fifteen minutes ago and I'm gonna take a nap."

"Do you want me to come and slip (sleep) wid you?"

"Are you serious?" I asked.

"Yeah."

"Okay," I answered with a smile.

POISON RUNNING FREE

Shit, I was starving too. So I fell asleep on him the first time, but if I fall asleep this time, I'll take the blame because I already told him that I wanted to take a nap.

**VENOMOUS MINDS 2**

## "PROMISES"

*LIFE IS FULL OF PROMISES AND DREAMS OF ALL SORTS*

*THINK INTELLECTUALLY; MAKE USE OF YOUR THOUGHTS*

I quickly took a shower because the last thing that you would want a man to remember you for is your musty female parts; it's a complete turn off. Plus, it'll look a little strange if I had a bowl of sliced lemons next to my bed – to cut the fish scent.

The hygiene thing goes for the men too, because seeing shit stains smeared up the back of a grown man's briefs is the ultimate turn off. Other than condoms, they should always keep wet wipes in their wallets.

I lotioned my entire body and threw on a pair of shorts and a tee.

POISON RUNNING FREE

BUZZ!

"Damn this man's fast," I muttered and looked in the mirror to make sure that I was looking good and of course, to see if there was any boo-boo in my eyes. And yes, never letting me down, there were two nice chunks in both corners. I quickly dug them out with a piece of tissue.

"Good morning," he said as he stepped in from the cold air.

"Yeah - did you fly here?" was my ill-mannered response.

"No. Why do you say dat?"

"Because you got here soooo quick."

"You tink so? I ate breakfast and even had time to smoke half a joint," Teddy mentioned.

"Whatever. I didn't ask you all that."

I turned on the television as we got comfy on the love seat. For several moments we sat quietly and just watched a show – nothing in particular.

"I taught (thought) you were gonna take a nap," he said, breaking the silence. I pretended not to hear him.

"Nishi!" Teddy somewhat shouted my name to get my attention.

"What?" He was so gullible sometimes.

"I taught you wanted to slip?"

"I did, but now you're here so I'll keep you company."

"You could keep me company while you slippin'," Teddy added.

"Gimme a break with that weak ass line. I could see if you just came out and said, 'Nishi let's go lay down.'"

POISON RUNNING FREE

"Fine....Nishi let's go lay down," he laughed.

"What's the rush?" I asked.

"Gyul, you play too much," he complained.

I rolled my eyes at him.

"There's a time for everyting," he added.

"Alright. Okay," I took a deep breath and stood up.

Halfway up the stairs, I turned to look behind me and discovered he wasn't there.

"Teddy! Where are you?" I stopped and shouted.

"Right haye!" he yelled from the kitchen doorway.

What are you doin' in the kitchen. This ain't no BREAKFAST AND THEN BED.

"Downstairs right?" Teddy asked.

**VENOMOUS MINDS 2**

"No-o-o. Come on," I instructed and waited for him to catch up.

This was the first time that Teddy had been in my room. Well, upstairs period. He removed his sweater and pants, but left on his boxers.

"Waye's dee batroom (Where's the bathroom)?" he asked.

"It's the one with the glass door."

He relieved himself and returned to my room moments later.

"Aren't you gonna take off you clothes?" he asked.

"No. For what?" I asked innocently.

"See what me talkin' about, you play too much," he became irritated again.

"Shut up! I'll take 'em off," I snapped.

POISON RUNNING FREE

He laid back and made himself comfortable. With one garment still on, I jumped into the bed and got beneath the covers.

"What's with dee shut (shirt)?" Once again he was annoyed.

"It's cold in here."

"I'll keep you warm. Just take dee shut off," he said.

By 12:00 p.m. that afternoon, we were done and still had enough time for a two hour nap...

*******

Being that I was no longer attending school, Teddy visited me almost daily. If he didn't stop by during the day, he'd visit me in the night. During this time we grew closer and began to feel more comfortable around one another.

"Nishi can you do sometin (something) for me pliz (please)?"

"It depends on what it is. I hope you don't want something to drink, because I'm not going back downstairs," I clearly stated during one of his day visits.

"I don't want you to go anyway and I don't want anyting to drink."

"So what'ta you want then?" I raised my left eyebrow.

Without saying another word, he gently placed his hand on the back of my head and slowly pushed it downward as he squatted in front of me.

"Oh I don't think so!" I snatched his hand off of my head.

"But why not? We talked about it," he said, with a whine in his voice.

"No. You talked about it and I just listened," I reminded him.

POISON RUNNING FREE

"Pliz?" he begged. "I did it for you."

"That's YOUR business. You did it because YOU wanted to."

"But you said you would tink about it."

"I did and I'm letting you know now – I'm not doing it!"

"Pliz Nishi. You don't have to do it long. Just put you mowt (mouth) on it," Teddy insisted.

"Nope!"

"Come on!" he continue to beg. Teddy began to adjust himself on the bed.

"Just close you eyes and open you mowt. You don't have to look if you don't want."

He changed his position and was now hunched over my face.

VENOMOUS MINDS 2

"I can just picture you tellin' MooMoo that I gave you a blow job."

"Pliz gyul! Why would I do dat? This is between me and you."

"Oh and our first time together wasn't. Move. Move from over me."

I pushed his abdomen away from my face.

"Every time I think about that shit, it makes me sick to my stomach. I'll really be your slut if I do this," I angrily voiced.

"Every time me ask you to do dis for me, it's always some shit," he snarled.

For several moments I just laid there.

"Alright... I'll do it, but I need the sheets."

"For what?" Teddy asked.

POISON RUNNING FREE

"To cover my face so that you won't see me," I explained.

"That's taken all dee fun from it." He shook his head for emphasis.

"Look! Are you gonna give me the sheet or what?" He reluctantly handed me the flat sheet and I covered my head.

Slowly, I reached for his penis with my right hand, but to my disliking, there was some light still shining in; so, with my left hand I blocked the ray of light. Immediately, after placing my mouth over the tip of his penis he moaned.

"Ahhhhh!"

I removed his penis from between my lips.

"What you stoppin' foe?" he asked as he snatched the sheet off my head.

VENOMOUS MINDS 2

"Because you're makin' noise!" I said while holding onto his manhood.

"Alright! I won't make any noises." He quickly threw the sheet back over my head.

I slowly lifted his manhood and placed it back, but barely, in my mouth.

"Ummmm! Ah.....!" He grew conscious of his moans and right away brought them to a halt.

Repositioning his penis caused him to throw his head back. I stuck my tongue out to lick his urethral opening; the taste was slightly bitter. Bitter to me but sweet for him. This was indeed, a bittersweet moment.

As I became more comfortable with this oral act, I aggressively groped his scrotum. In my hand, it felt warm and silky. I then released the shaft of his penis and commenced to sucking on his testicles. Within moments, I reverted back to Teddy's penis and pushed his reproductive organ further down my salivated throat. Teddy then gently applied some pressure to the back of my head. Apparently, he had recognized my liberated participation and began to pump harder, which caused his penis to touch the back of my throat.

OOOOWAAAH! I gagged. With a quickness, I snatched his uncircumcised penis out of my mouth.

"Wait! You pushin' it in too far," I snapped.

His eager act had somewhat killed the mood.

"I'm sorry. It just felt so good and I didn't want you to stop."

"Well if you keep it up, I'm gonna throw up on your ass," I expressed.

"Alright. I'll do it easier," he promised.

"Don't do it at all - I know what to do," I fussed.

VENOMOUS MINDS 2

We resumed our position. At this point, I was extremely comfortable because I was no longer covered with the sheet. Seconds into it, Teddy switched things up a bit by gripping the headboard. I didn't care too much for this position because with every pump his penis would leave my suckling lips unlike before. Something had to give, so I clutched his buttocks and plunged his pelvis closer to my face.

"Oooowaaah!" I gagged again, but this time I was able to continue with the maneuver.

"Umm! Uhhh! Uhhh! Umm!" Teddy sensually moaned repeatedly.

"Nishi. Can I come in you mowt?" he managed to groan. WHAT?!!!

Now hold on....I don't recall me mentioning anything about being thirsty. With his penis still lodged

POISON RUNNING FREE

between my lips. I shook my head frantically and muttered, "Uhn! Uhn!"

"Pliz!" he begged.

"Uhn! Uhn!" I shook my head no again.

"Pli-i-z-z! Huuuuuuuh!" Teddy's face turned red.

"Eep!" I pulled back.

Some of Teddy's liquid love had squirted to the back of my throat. To the bathroom I ran. Trying to rid my throat of Teddy's reproductive fluid, I gargled with warm water for several minutes before returning to my room.

"EEEWWWW! Why is the sheet so wet?" I quickly threw it to the side.

"It's not wet over haye (here)," Teddy said, checking his side of the bed.

"Damn! I got this shit all on me too."

VENOMOUS MINDS 2

Some sperm had landed on my chest directly beneath my chin. Instead of running back to the bathroom, I used the tee-shirt that I'd been wearing to wipe away the excess semen.

"Yeah! I bet you're happy now. And just to let you know, that was your Christmas present," I stated firmly.

Teddy rolled over and hugged me tightly. Having completed my "jawz-ercise" and tasting his condensed milk, I laid my weary body down and curled up under him.

"I love you Nishi....only if you knew how much."

That was the first time he had ever told ME that he loved me. I remained silent, buried my head in his chest and returned the tight hug.

"But next time move you teet (your teeth) out of dee way!"

******

POISON RUNNING FREE

That Christmas, Teddy and I exchanged gifts on Christmas Eve because he wanted to be with his son on Christmas Day, which was understandable.

Very nice! I was shocked. Teddy had bought me an 18 karat herring bone necklace. It was ½ an inch wide, approximately 20" long and shaped in the form of a heart. It was beautiful!

"Thank you Mr. Ted," I said, while carefully placing the necklace back in its case.

"Okay - now you open yours!" *Lord, I hope he likes his gift*, I thought to myself as he untied the bow. Shit - he better like it. This was three years' worth of savings. When he opened the box and tossed the paper, his face lit up. Great! He likes it.

"Thank you Nishi. I like it. It's nice." I had given him a black wool sweater trimmed with leather. We then exchanged kisses.

"You're welcome," I smiled.

"Is you mudda (mother) haye?" Teddy asked while placing his sweater back in the box.

"Nah. She's out doing some last minute shopping," I answered.

We sat and talked for a bit, but throughout the duration of his visit he constantly glanced at his watch. Before we knew it, it was almost 10:00.

"Let me go; it's getting late. Haye, give this to you mudda." He handed me a joint. I took it and placed it on top of my gift. Despite my disapproval, they remained smoking partners.

"So I'll see you after Christmas, right?" I asked as I walked him to the door.

"Yeah, we'll see," he replied nonchalantly while zipping up his jacket.

POISON RUNNING FREE

What?!

"What do you mean we'll see?" I asked, annoyed.

"I'll try. I have a lot to do over dee vacation," he explained.

"Alright," I let it go. After all it was Christmas. I kissed him good night and closed the door...

Christmas Day was here and so was my entire family. We exchanged gifts, as well as joyful memories. Once again we were a family. I called my partner in crime to see what she was up to.

"Hey shorty, Merry Christmas," I greeted Sandra.

"Thank you. Same to you," she replied.

"So did your mother like her raincoat?" I asked.

"No doubt. No doubt. And it fits her perfectly too. Thank God I bought that extra-large."

VENOMOUS MINDS 2

"So what did you get?" I asked.

"Nish, Christmas is for kids," Sandra lightly chastised me.

"Whatever! So what did you get for your nephew?"

"Oh - I bought that spoiled brat a Nintendo 64. Now he's the one who got everything. I know Toys R Us is happy," she commented.

"Well you did say that Christmas is for the churin' right? So there," I responded.

"Did Teddy like his gift?"

"Yeah he did."

"I hope the sleeves are long enough for that tall skinny motherf...." Sandra began to say.

"Don't even!" I defended him.

POISON RUNNING FREE

"You just don't want me to go there `cause you're in love. Nish is in love!" she yelled.

"Whatever," I disregarded her statement.

"What did he get you?" she asked.

"I got a gold herring bone necklace."

"Say word? Is it the big or small pattern?" Sandra asked.

"Big."

"Word? I saw that shit in the mall and it was like three bucks."

Sandra spoke with a lot of slang. If she said a buck and change, that simply meant one hundred and some odd dollars.

VENOMOUS MINDS 2

"It's good that you both liked each other's gifts. Shit - he needs to spend money like that on you all the time with all the lying that he's done," Sandra continued.

"You're sick," I responded.

"Nah...but seriously Nish, I hope that you and he make it, because I know you really care about this clown and it seems like he cares for you too. I wish you two the best."

Sandra may have been a bit of a tomboy, but deep down inside she had a soft side that many didn't see. She was the real deal. My confidant, my soul sistah and my friend to the end. Sandra was the only person that I had categorized as being my true friend.

"Thank you shorty," I wiped the tears from my eyes and proceeded to change the subject.

POISON RUNNING FREE

Page 153

"No diggity doubt." Oh here we go again with the slang.

"So what did Rumps get for you?"

"Nothing. He said that he didn't have to wait until the 25th of December to celebrate Christmas or any holiday, because he did it every day by loving himself and the others that surround him. Rumps firmly believes that this is just a way to make money before the year end."

"I respect that and it's true if you really think about it."

"Yeah it's true. But still, that's a real dread for yuh...and let me tell you, he doesn't like to be called a dread," Sandra then added.

"Why? What did he vindicate this time?"

"He said he wasn't the type of person who walked around putting fear in people's hearts, so why should he

VENOMOUS MINDS 2

accept that term. Then he said, 'I am a Rasta. A man made by God that believes highly in nature,'" Sandra explained. I could tell that she and Rasta Rumps had engaged in some deep seeded conversation, which was cool.

"Nish, when he said that, I asked him what type of nature, WEED?"

We both broke out laughing. Rumps was also a chronic pot head, just like Teddy and just like my mother.

"Well while we're on stories, let me tell you this one," I chuckled.

"Nish, what did you do?"

"Nothing! Hold up - let me tell you."

I took a deep breath.

"Remember the morning when I told you that Teddy came over and we had sex again?"

POISON RUNNING FREE

"Yeah," Sandra responded.

"Girl, I tasted something that I had never tasted before."

BADOOOOM! Sandra dropped her phone.

"Hello! Hello!" I kept saying.

Then all of a sudden I heard loud screaming in her background.

"Uhhhhh! No! No! No! No! No you didn't. Oh my God!"

After hearing her screams for about two minutes straight, she FINALLY regained her senses.

"Sandra what's wrong with you?" I asked while laughing.

"Nishi, tell me you didn't?"

"Didn't what?" I asked, holding back the laughter.

VENOMOUS MINDS 2

"Tell me you didn't do what I think you did?"

"Will you just shut up and let me finish?" I told her.

"Alright go ahead....please Lord," she mumbled.

"He asked me to do him a favor and of course...."

"Ohhhhhhhhh!" Sandra began screaming to the top of her lungs again.

"Look, do you want me to tell you or what?" I asked the drama queen.

"I can't help it," she cried out.

"Anywaaaay! I asked him what is it that he wanted, then he asked me if ...."

I paused a second, waiting for Sandra's scream.

"If what? Come on!" she shouted.

"If I could perform oral sex for him."

POISON RUNNING FREE

BADOOOM! There went the phone again

Sandra was my girl and all, but this chick had some serious issues. For another two minutes she temporarily lost her mind.

"Nishi, I can't believe you!" She returned to the phone and shouted.

"What? It wasn't all that bad."

"Wasn't all that bad?! Nish, you put his dick in your mouth!"

"AND???" I replied.

"Oh my God!" Sandra blurted.

"In the beginning, I was a little scared, but a few gags later, I was alright."

"Nishi, I would have never in a million years expected for YOU to do something like that," she expressed.

"Why do you say that?"

"Cause, Miss Stuck-Up from back in the day. Please! You don't even like when a person coughs near you, never mind sucking dick. Ohhhhhhhh!" Sandra cried out again.

"Correction! It was Miss Confident and for your information I was simply pleasing my man."

"Well I guess my man will never be pleased then," Sandra stated.

"Damn! I feel sorry for Rumps," I clowned.

"Please! Rumps ain't even get a kiss from me yet and probably won't," Sandra added.

"Anyway, that's not all," I said to her.

POISON RUNNING FREE

The best was yet to come.

"Lord...what else did you do? Did you suck his toes too?" Sandra joked.

"No....I swallowed some of it."

"N-i-s-h-i-i-i-i!" she howled.

"Yep! And it tasted like soap. Now top THAT story," I dared her.

"Yoooooooooo! I KNOW you in love now! You can't tell me that you don't love that punk!"

I sang to the beat of one of Tina Turner's greatest hits.

"You're sick. I'm not even gonna front. You got that one. Yo let me go, `cause I hear my moms callin' me. She probably wants me to go to the store for her. I'll check back with you later."

"Alright."

"Later penis breath," Sandra sarcastically added.

"Don't be a hater," I laughed. "Later shorty."

*"NOTHING BUT HIS FOOL"*

*WE'RE BACK TOGETHER BUT I HAVEN'T HEARD FROM HIM IN A WHILE*

*AT LEAST I KNOW IT'S NOT BECAUSE OF ANOTHER WOMAN*

*HE SAID THAT I'M THE ONLY ONE*

Three days had passed and not a word from Teddy. He'll call tomorrow though – I'm sure. He's probably taking care of his business like he said he would be. Four days later, I got in the van and drove past his apartment. Okay, well at least I know he's still alive because his van wasn't parked there earlier. I'm sure he'll bring in the New Year with me.

As I approached the traffic light, something told me to look in my rear view mirror. To my surprise, Teddy had left the building and was walking towards his van. My man is coming to see me, I thought. Wait - who's that with him? Someone of a small statue was walking alongside him. Hurry up light! My plan was to go around the block and come back around. Could it be her? Could it be THE MooMoo?

VROOOOOM! I hit the gas, but by the time I made it back around, Mr. Slick had already pulled off.

That very same night, Sandra called me around 11:30.

"Yo Nish, I saw your man on my block earlier. I was outside talkin' with my neighbors and I saw him pull up and park. I walked towards his van thinkin' the person in the passenger seat was you, but as the door opened and the person's foot touched the ground, I knew it wasn't you. The shoes. This chick had on some old granny looking shoes that were all crushed down on the back."

"And what did you do?" I asked her.

POISON RUNNING FREE

"I turned away and went in the opposite direction. Yo, he had MooMoo with him. They went into this Grenadian guy's house two doors away from me. I think he was having a party or something 'cause not too long after they had gotten there, other people started to pour in," she explained.

Throughout the entire time Sandra was telling her story, I was listening, but had zoned out a bit. *You have time to go to parties, but you can't call or stop by to see me,* I fumed to myself.

"Nishi, you there?" Sandra asked.

"Yeah - I'm still here. You know I haven't spoken to or seen him since Christmas Eve?"

"Word? That's fucked up! Chump! He ain't no man, he's a fuckin' punk!" Sandra angrily spoke.

"It's okay," I said.

VENOMOUS MINDS 2

"Nish, what you gonna do?"

"Nothing," I said.

"I know you. And plus I can hear it in your voice."

"I SAID NOTHIN'!" I said, raising my voice. "Anyway let me go."

"Alright. Later," Sandra said as we hung up.

Sandra knew me like the back of her hand. She could tell that I was upset from the way I was NOT talking; I simply wanted Teddy to know he wasn't going to play me over and over again. So at 3:00am when my alarm sounded, I got up, got dressed and went up the road. Me writing him a letter and leaving the note on his van was a sure way of getting his attention...

\*\*\*\*\*\*

Being that Renee' was pregnant again, Paul had no reason to monitor her every move. Her visits with the

POISON RUNNING FREE

family now lasted several hours; this allowed Renee' and I to catch up on our stories.

RING! RING!

Renee's pregnant ass ran to answer the phone. Our answering machine was back.

"Nishi it was Teddy. He said that he's around the corner at the pay phone and to come outside because he wants to talk to you."

"Did he sound mad?" I anxiously questioned Renee'.

"He sounded okay to me. Why?" Renee' asked.

"Girl I wrote him a nasty letter and that's what he wants to talk to me about."

"So why should he be mad? It's only a letter." Poor thing, she just didn't understand.

"Renee'....I wrote the letter ON his van."

VENOMOUS MINDS 2

"You mean, you wrote on the man's van?" Renee asked, her eyes spread wide.

"Yes."

"That's wrong Nish! Why did you do some shit like that?" Renee' frowned.

"I'll explain later. Come with me outside just in case he acts stupid."

Renee' grabbed her coat and ran towards the kitchen.

As she and I grew closer to the front door, Renee reached beneath her ¾ length tweed coat.

"What are you doing?" I watched her strangely.

"I went to get a knife," she seriously stated. Prison had made the girl rougher.

POISON RUNNING FREE

"Don't come out with me. Just watch from the door," I told her. But by then Teddy was standing at the bottom of the stairs, looking up at me.

"Come out haye so I can talk to you," he ordered. I descended the stairs slowly and stopped two steps before reaching the bottom.

"What?" I asked with a slight attitude.

"Come. Let's take a walk. I'm not gonna do you anyting." With that comment, I should have run back inside the house, but I didn't. I took the walk with him...

As Teddy and I progressed further away from the house, I looked back after hearing the clinking sound of a gate closing. Slowly walking towards us was Renee'.

"Why did you write on me vahn?" Teddy asked me calmly.

"I don't know what you're talkin' about," I responded.

Instantly, he swung at me. Motherfuck! Bitch ass....you tryin' to sneak me? I ducked and took my boxer's stance.

"Come on! Bastard!" I angrily spoke.

CLICK! CLICK! CLICK! CLICK! CLICK!

It was Renee'. She was running towards us with her noisy boots.

"What's up Renee'?" Teddy greeted her as if nothing was going on.

"Hi Teddy," Renee spoke back with the same demeanor.

Before anyone one of us could say something or do something....PLINK! PLINK!

POISON RUNNING FREE

The damn knife fell from beneath Renee's jacket and, to make matters worse, it was a BUTTER knife.

"Renee' I know you didn't bring that for me right?" Teddy asked with a smile.

"Uhn Uhn!" she grunted and shook her head no.

Renee' wasn't quite the roughneck after all. She still had a lot to learn about being a criminal.

Teddy grabbed my hand and pulled me towards him.

"You see these long nails of yours. Next time you touch me vahn I'm gonna break 'em off along with you fingers." He bent my fingers while talking.

"Get off my hand!"

"You hear what I said gyul?" He bent them even more.

"Yes. Now let me go bitch!" I shouted.

VENOMOUS MINDS 2

"You still talkin' shit?" He attempted to grab me again, but I dodged him and ran.

The 6' 2", 150 lbs. feather weight caught up with me in four leaps.

"Nishi, seriously, don't do that again. I don't care how mahd (mad) you get. Stuff like dat will only push me away," Teddy expressed as we approached the house.

"I'm going inside! It's getting cold out here and my daughter's looking for me," Renee said. The roughneck went inside with her silverware.

"I don't care if I push you away. I hope that I push you straight back to Grenada. Didn't you read my letter?" I asked sarcastically. The letter read:

*Fuck you you lying bastard. Why don't you take your ass back to Grenada!*

POISON RUNNING FREE

I fit that on the entire driver's side, in HUGE print in black marker. Boy did it show up nicely against that powder blue high gloss enamel paint job of his.

"Fuck you gyul!" Again he tightly squeezed my hand.

I took both Renee' and Teddy home later that evening.

"Who wants to go first?" I asked.

"I'll go first because my daughter is sleepy and I'm not trying to carry her inside," Renee' answered.

"Okay," I said and headed for Canarsie, Brooklyn.

"So did you two straighten out everything?" Renee' inquired half way through the ride.

"NO... because Nishi listens to other piple (people) and that's what got she so upset in dee fust (first) place," Teddy responded immediately.

"Other people like who? Please ...what are you talking about?" I played dumb.

"You li'ckle (little) bitch of a friend on 96th street," he snapped.

"Whatever!"

"I know she see me wid Meryl," Teddy admitted.

"And was she NOT supposed to tell me?" I spoke loudly.

"Shushhhhh! Tameera's sleeping," Renee whispered.

"Sorry!" I apologized. I hadn't realized that my little cousin had fallen asleep.

"No - she wasn't supposed to tell you, 'cause look at what she statted (started). And she doesn't even know what she's talking about, because I didn't want Meryl to come wid me in dee fust place. Dee gyul forced she way into dee vahn as me tried to leave," Teddy explained.

*So that's why I only saw you walking towards the van at first*, I thought to myself. Damn. Now I felt stupid.

"Okay. That only explains Sandra's block incident, but why haven't I spoken to you in what....? FOUR DAYS?" I questioned him.

"I don't know. I just didn't feel like comin' out," Teddy replied.

He was so full of shit! How can you go from spending almost every day with a person and announcing you love them to 'I JUST DIDN'T FEEL LIKE COMING OUT?'

"Bullshit!" I roared.

"I don't know about you two, but I do know one thing. This craziness needs to stop!" Renee' counseled us.

"She statted it. She and she dahm (damn) friend."

VENOMOUS MINDS 2

"Well - I really don't know who started what, but from the looks of that house right there, I am home," Renee pointed out.

"Teddy can you please do me a favor and open these middle doors so I won't hit Tameera's head while carrying her out," Renee asked for assistance.

"You need help gettin' down?" Teddy asked her.

"Nah, I got it. Thanks."

"Nish, thanks. I'll call you tomorrow. Teddy stay cool!" Renee' said and walked towards her basement apartment's front door.

The excitement had worn me out, so after dropping Teddy off, I went straight home and to bed...

******

Winter break was over, a new year had begun and school was back in session.

POISON RUNNING FREE

"Stop! Give it back to me! Gimme my game back! Nishi tell Christopher to give me my game!" one kid shouted.

"I got Nintendo and my brother got a remote control car. My grandma bought me three Power Rangers and she ...Move! You're squishing me!" another kid shouted, suddenly going from sharing his happy Christmas moments to quarreling with a school mate.

"Well move your book bag then!" another kid argued.

"LOOK!" I shouted out. I now had their undivided attention.

"If the toy doesn't belong to you - give it back! And make space for one another so that no one is squished. If you all don't listen – YOU WILL WALK!" I warned the group.

VENOMOUS MINDS 2

"ST-O-P-P-P!" one kid shouted.

"What did I just say ...now I don't wanna hear another sound from y'all!"

I put a stop to the madness once and for all. Didn't feel like comin' out here in this damn snow anyway. Should'a called in sick. And why am I so tired?

"Hey Ree. How's things? How's the baby coming along?" I phoned her one evening. She was now two and a half months pregnant and already starting to show.

"I'm fine, but the doctors said something about me having a lot of fluid," she said, sounding worried.

"Well - that's better than having NO fluid, 'cause we don't want another dry birth now do we?"

"You right about that shit," Renee' somewhat laughed.

POISON RUNNING FREE

"Well I just called to see how things were coming along with the baby and all."

"Yeah, everything's fine. What's up with you and Teddy? Y'all okay?" she asked.

"I guess so, but these days I haven't been in the mood for his company. My head's been hurting me a lot and I don't get headaches like that; plus, I've been sleeping a lot too," I explained to her.

"Girl...you sound like you're pregnant. That's the same way I felt this time when I got pregnant," she stated.

"Well - we'll know by next week, because that's when my period is supposed to come," I told her.

"That'll be some shit. Both of us being pregnant together like our mothers', but instead of our kids being days apart - they'll be months apart," Renee' admired.

VENOMOUS MINDS 2

"Yeah …That WOULD be some shit. Anyway, let me go to bed. Gotta get up early in the morning to make that money for the massah."

"You're so stupid," Renee laughed. "But seriously Nish. I don't think you should have stopped going to college for this shit. Your mother could have found someone to drive for her….she just didn't want to. Your mother knew what she was doing and I think that's real fucked up of her," Renee' stated in disgust.

"But I couldn't leave her hanging like that Ree," I reasoned.

"Fuck that shit Nishi," Renee spat. "She lived her life. It's time for you to live yours. You were on the right track, but NO-O-O…here she comes with her sad stories. Personally, I think you should have gone away to school; I bet then she would have found a driver. And another thing," she continued on her rant, "you said you spent your

POISON RUNNING FREE

entire Pell and Tap checks on the van. Should'a left that money in YOUR pocket."

"I did it because it's my mother and plus, I drive the van like it's mine anyway," I explained.

"But it's NOT your van," Renee said. "Like I said, you should have kept that money for a rainy day Nish. Don't ever say I never told you so."

"Well girl, I wanna get a good night's rest so I can deal with those noisy ass brats tomorrow morning," I said, cutting the conversation. "I'll talk to you later during the week."

"Alright Nish - later!"

Although, Renee' HAD made some very valid points, this was MY mother and no matter what, I was gonna be there for her.

VENOMOUS MINDS 2

One evening that following week, I initiated a conference call.

"Ree are you there?" I asked.

"Yeah I'm here," she responded.

"Sandra are you there?" I then asked.

"Yeah I'm here too," Sandra replied.

"What's up Sandra?" Renee' greeted.

"Hey Ree. How's things?"

"Alright I guess. I'm home so that's a start."

"No doubt! No doubt! So how's the baby....or should I say babies?" Sandra asked.

"Both are fine."

"Good. So do you have to go back to Maryland for court or anything like that?" Sandra asked.

POISON RUNNING FREE

"Nah. I'm done. They said as long as I don't get into any trouble during my probationary period then my case is automatically closed, but I still have to report to my parole officer every week for the next three years," she explained.

"Well, that's not too bad and like you said, the main thing is that you're out. It's good to hear your voice though," Sandra expressed.

"Appreciate it. Thanks Sandra," Renee' responded.

"Okay... now that you two have become reacquainted, can I state the purpose of this call?" I commented.

"Go ahead, 'cause I know it has something to do with Teddy," Sandra blatantly said.

"Renee' remember when I spoke to you last week and said that I was sleeping a lot and that I kept getting those frequent headaches?" I started out.

**VENOMOUS MINDS 2**

"Yeah," Renee' responded.

"You may be right – because my period hasn't come yet," I stated.

"Say Word!" Sandra voiced in shock.

"For real? Does Teddy know?" Renee' asked.

"Nah, I wanted to mention it to him last night when he came over, but I didn't."

"Don't say another word `cause I'm gonna make an appointment for you to get a pregnancy test at the same place I had mine done. It's free and if you ARE pregnant, they'll tell you where to go for your prenatal visits and the whole nine yards," Renee' informed me.

"But I don't have any insurance," I explained to her.

"Please girl. There's ways around that. There's something called MEDICAID." Sandra chimed in.

"But isn't that welfare?" I asked.

"Yeah - to a certain extent. Nishi, DO YOU HAVE INSURANCE?" Renee' spoke forcefully.

"No."

"Well then - there's your answer," Renee' concluded, proving her point.

"Hold up! Hold up! We ain't even sure she's pregnant yet," Sandra jumped in.

"We'll know by tomorrow morning though. Nishi, I'm gonna make an appointment for you as soon as we get off the phone."

Renee' was obviously the person in charge. She had this entire project broken down to a science.

"Okay - so tomorrow when I finish the morning run, we'll go. I'll come and pick you up, like around 9:30. Is that okay?" I asked Renee.

VENOMOUS MINDS 2

"Yeah, I just have to let Paul know he's gonna have to stay with Tameera for a while and I hope it won't be any shit with him. If so, I'll just bring her with me."

"So Nish, on the way to pick up Renee', you can pass to pick me up right?" Sandra asked.

"Okay. So Sandra you be ready at 9:20, I'll pick you up first," I said.

"Shit! I'll be ready at 8:20." Sandra was obviously in a hurry to hear the results.

"You're a foolish child Sandra. Alright ladies, I shall see you both in the morning," I said, closing the conversation.

"Alright. Later," Renee' hung up.

"Later," Sandra hung up right behind her.

POISON RUNNING FREE

*Shit,* I thought to myself. *I wonder if I really AM pregnant. He did pull out, but then again - so did cheese head Mike...*

The next morning we arrived at the testing center a little before 10:00. The three of us took a seat as I completed the pertinent paper work.

"Nishi. You scared?" Renee' asked.

"No, but if I am pregnant - I'll be happy," I responded.

"That's all I wanted to hear," Renee' smiled and sat back.

"For real," Sandra then added.

By their responses, I could tell these two were going to be very supportive.

"Nishelle Maron?" the nurse called.

VENOMOUS MINDS 2

"Yes," I answered.

"Can you follow me please?" she asked.

I got up and entered one of the many examining rooms. Some seven minutes later, I returned to the waiting area.

"What did she say? Are you?" Sandra grilled me.

"Relax - they just took my urine sample. Damn, can a sister take a piss?" I sarcastically responded. Renee' and Sandra both chuckled. The three of us sat anxiously waiting.

"Nishelle Maron!" FINALLY! That same nurse called me back into the room.

"Okay Nishelle, according to your paperwork you're a Pisces." the nurse said as she smiled.

"Yes I am."

"Good people!" she then added.

POISON RUNNING FREE

"You're right ...we're GREAT people!" I praised my zodiac sign.

"I'm gonna have to agree with you on that one, 'cause I'm a Pisces also." She widened her smile.

"Oh okay. Lot of fish in here huh?" I made a joke.

*Cut the small talk lady*! She was nice and all, but come on, I wanted to know my results.

"Well Ms. Pisces. You're definitely pregnant," the nurse said, finally giving me the news. I grinned from ear to ear.

"Wow! What a huge smile. I'm going to assume that you're happy with this pregnancy and you're keeping it?" she inquired.

"Yep!"

"Wonderful! Here are your results. Now on your way out I want you to stop at the front desk and the young lady there will instruct you on where to go for your prenatal visits. Take care and good luck with your baby," she shook my hand.

"Thank you." Pleased with the outcome, I re-entered the waiting room once again to find Sandra and Renee staring me down. .

"Well?!" they spoke simultaneously.

"I am," I smiled.

"YES!" they shouted while hugging me.

"Nishi's gonna have a little Ted-d-d-dy! Nishi's gonna have a little Ted-d-d-dy!" Renee' harmonized.

"Wait a minute y'all, I have to get this paper from the receptionist and then we can go," I said as I peeled away from their hold.

On the way to the van, they screamed and shouted in joy.

POISON RUNNING FREE

"When are you tellin' Teddy?" Renee' asked.

"I don't know. In a way, I'm kind of scared," I admitted.

"Why? Y'all been going together for over three years now and you're scared?" Renee' asked.

"Cause....I don't know how he's going to react to this news."

"Please! That bitch better be happy like the rest of us AND he better start savin' up for some milk and Pampers," Sandra jumped in.

"I'll tell him. Do you think that he's coming over tonight?" Renee' asked.

"I don't know. It's hard to tell with him. He comes when he feels like it," I responded.

"Well. I'll go on the run with you this afternoon to ask him if he's gonna come," Renee offered, not giving up.

VENOMOUS MINDS 2

"Damn Ree. You aint stoppin' are you?" Sandra voiced.

"Stoppin' for what? We are talking about a baby here in case you haven't noticed," Renee' firmly answered Sandra.

"Okay! You ain't gotta chew my head off – shit! I'm with you on that 100%." Sandra grew somewhat offended, but was in total agreement with my cousin.

"I'm sorry... I didn't mean to say it like that. It's just that he better not act stupid. You know how these men get," Renee' explained.

"Don't mess with Ree 'cause she might pull out a butter knife," I joked.

While waiting at the school for the first set of kids to come out that afternoon, Teddy drove up as scheduled.

"Nish that's Teddy's van right?" Renee' asked.

POISON RUNNING FREE

"Yeah," I answered.

"Alright. I'll be right back," Renee' quickly jumped out of the van.

"Nish why is it that you always have to wait so long for these same two kids to come out?" Sandra asked.

"I know right," I answered while watching Renee and Teddy as they spoke outside of his van.

"What's up with that?" Sandra continued.

"I don't know, but every year it's the same thing and I know it's not the teacher this time, 'cause they couldn't possibly have had the same teacher for the last 3 years," I said.

"Okay ...he said that he'll be there tonight," Renee' said as she climbed back in the front seat of the van.

"Oh God! Now I'm really nervous," I explained.

"Don't even worry about it Nish, 'cause I already told you, I'm going to do all the talking and when I'm done – I'm going home. I've been out here all day with y'all asses," Renee laughed.

*******

All of 8:00 p.m. was approaching and Renee was starting to complain about the time. Hurry up Teddy! I grew jumpy. Watching back to back episodes of A Different World grew boring after a while.

Finally, the bell rang. Teddy walked in lookin' AND smellin' all good. He no longer had that wolf man appearance and was doing a good job at maintaining the gentleman look since the first hair cut that I had given him – that fro had to go.

He and I took a seat in the living room and some moments later Sandra joined us.

"What's up Teddy?" Sandra respectfully greeted him. Renee' was literally two steps behind her.

"Hey coolie bwaaoy! I see you got a haircut. Did you have your hair like that earlier?" Renee' asked. (The term "coolie" is used in the Caribbean, referring to individuals that had softer textured hair that was easier to manage, also known as "nice hair." Such individuals are of the Indian descent.)

"Yeah, but I had a hat on," Teddy answered.

"Right-t-t-t! I knew was something different. Anyway how was work?" Renee' procrastinated a bit.

"It was okay," he said.

"Well…." Renee paused. "My dear cousin here is a little scared to tell you that you are going to have a baby."

He looked at me and smiled.

VENOMOUS MINDS 2

"So what do you have to say about that?" Renee' boldly asked him.

"That's good - I'm happy," he answered, still smiling.

"So you're okay with it?" she rephrased her question.

"Yeah, I'm happy if Nishi's happy. I kind'a had a fillin' that she was anyway," he admitted.

"Oh and why do you say that?" Renee' asked.

"'Cause lately when I come over to see she, she act sometimeish (moody) and always slippin' (sleeping)," he explained.

"Nish are you satisfied with his answer?" Renee' then turned and faced me.

"Yeah," I said and shook my head.

"Good. Now take me home!" Renee' ordered.

POISON RUNNING FREE

"Yeah. You can drop me too!" Sandra added. As my partners in crime gathered their belongings, Teddy and I exchanged thoughts on our unborn child.

"You're going with me right?" I asked him.

"Yeah," he responded.

Renee' and Sandra sat on the first row seat and Teddy sat in the passenger seat next to me.

"I know this baby is going to be cute and I hope it's a boy. If she has a boy, he'll be so-o cute," Renee' stressed.

"Nah, you got it all wrong. It should be a girl," Sandra joined in.

"Why? So she could be a damn tomboy like you and her mamma," Renee' snapped.

"You know it!" Sandra happily voiced.

VENOMOUS MINDS 2

"Please! Where is she gonna put the baby - on the back of that damn motorcycle?" Renee sarcastically asked.

"That's right! I'll have a biker car seat specially made for him or her," I bragged. Teddy looked at me and rolled his eyes.

"I don't blame you Teddy. I saw the look that you just gave her," Renee' sided with him.

After dropping them both off, Teddy and I went back to the house and seriously discussed our pregnancy. He rubbed my stomach and expressed to me how happy he was. He didn't stay long though, and deep down inside, I knew that the only reason he came over was because of Renee's request.

Some Friday's later, Sandra and I waited at the subway station for my mother to arrive.

POISON RUNNING FREE

"Nish there goes that chic!" Sandra pointed out. She had spotted an individual in the passenger side view mirror.

"What chic?" I asked in a relaxed tone.

"You know. What's her name? Teddy's girl!"

"Which one? The short one or the tall one?" I sat up to get a better look.

"The short one - she just came up to the van. Didn't you see her?" Sandra grew excited.

"No! And came up to which van? This one?" I looked hard at Sandra.

"Yeah. I was looking in the mirror to see if your mom's was coming and I saw her."

"Are you sure that's her?" I asked.

"Nish. I was in the girl's house. Yes, I'm sure."

VENOMOUS MINDS 2

By now MooMoo had passed the van and was at least a block away from where I was parked. I started the van and proceeded to catch up with her. Teddy's apartment building was in walking distance from the subway, so whatever I was gonna do, I had to do it quick.

Due to light traffic and a couple of red lights, MooMoo had already gotten closer to her building. Damn. This one caught me too. The intersecting traffic was moving like crazy and the light wasn't at all about to change, so what was I to do? I ran the light, crossed the double solid yellow lines and was now facing the oncoming traffic.

"Hurry up Nish, she's almost there!" Sandra voiced.

Just several steps before the two women could mount the sidewalk, I aggressively threw the van in front of them to block their path.

POISON RUNNING FREE

"What did you walk up on the van for?" I shouted through the passenger window.

"I can do what I want to!" she yelled back smartly. Yeah – this is MooMoo. I recognized her raspy voice and accent.

"Bitch! I will fuck you up," I challenged her. *Let's see how bad you are now! Talkin' all that shit on the phone.*

"Yo Nish. That bitch is running now. Haaaaaa!" Sandra exclaimed

"It's okay, `cause I'm gonna catch her ass before she gets in the building."

I threw the gear in park and we jumped out of the van. To my advantage, those parallel parked cars were so closely parked that MooMoo had to go around several of them before she could step onto the sidewalk. As for me and Sandra - we slid over the hood of a car.

"Now what was that bitch? Who you gonna kill when you see them?"

I jumped in her face as she approached her building's entrance. The rough and tough MooMoo didn't have anything to say. She simply stood there fumbling with her keys.

"Ahhh! She ain't got nothing to say now. PUNK ASS BITCH! She just like her man," Sandra spoke loudly as she circled around Meryl like a shark. We knew that she was nervous, because her hands were shaking so much she couldn't get the key into its slot.

Like a cornered stray animal, MooMoo turned to face her rival.

"Hi..remember me? I was at your house for Thanksgiving," Sandra laughed.

MooMoo looked, and then looked again. From the scowl on her face I knew she now recognized Sandra.

"Haaaaaa!" Sandra laughed loudly again.

"Look, I don't want any trouble from you," MooMoo stated.

Remember the taller person that was walking next to her? Well, turns out that the girl was her "little" sister. She was at least 6' 0" tall and 200 lbs. - a big heifer, but we didn't care.

"You sayin' that shit now `cause I'm in your fuckin' face," I said as I raised my fist.

Her monstrous sibling jumped in between us.

"YO-O-O! You ain't got nothing to do with this so take your big ass inside!" Sandra intervened.

VENOMOUS MINDS 2

"This is my sister and I'm not gonna let you hit her," Gigantor said as she boldly walked up to Sandra. Each time the sister moved, MooMoo would hide behind her.

"And I'm not gonna let you get all up in my friend's face either," I said to Gigantor.

Just when MooMoo thought that the coast was clear, Sandra swung at her.

"Don't touch me!" MooMoo broke bad.

"I'm not gonna TOUCH you. I'm just gonna fuck you up!" Sandra said and swung at her a second time. At this point the sister shoved me and ran after Sandra. I grabbed the sister back causing her to drop her bag.

"Fine, you wanna fight? I'm tired of you ass. I'm not going to let you two gang up on my sister," the BIG baby sister said. She had WAY more heart than MooMoo.

I pushed the big bitch with all my might.

POISON RUNNING FREE

"Nobody's ganging up on your sister and I know you better not push me again," I threatened, throwing up my hands - Tyson style.

"No! No! Don't fight wit dem!" Meryl shouted as she grabbed her little sister.

People were now starting to gather in front of the building.

"Let's go!" she yanked her sister's arm.

Quick thinking MooMoo caught the door with her bag as two other individuals exited the building.

"Nish come on. Let's go; mad people are passing by now and plus, all she got is damn mouth," Sandra suggested.

Sandra and I slowly backed away. We so did not get the action that we thought we'd get.

VENOMOUS MINDS 2

"BITCH! I WILL KILL YOU THE NEXT TIME THAT I SEE YOU!" Meryl shouted through the lobby door.

By then Sandra and I were already entering the van.

"FUCK YOU MOOMOO! AND YOU BETTER NOT LET ME CATCH YOU EITHER, CAUSE I'M ALWAYS READY!" Sandra returned the threat.

"Yo Nish that bitch is a punk. She had to hide behind her sister so we wouldn't fuck her up."

"Well at least I know how she looks now. Let's get outta here for real, 'cause I'm sure my mother's at the station by now."

Sure enough she was there, waiting and looking pissed. "What took you so damn long? Do you know how long I've been waiting out here in this damn cold? Fifteen fuckin' minutes," my mother vented.

"Traffic," I responded...

POISON RUNNING FREE

*"THINKING OF YESTERDAY"*

*ADULTS WE'VE BECOME*

*YESTERDAYS ARE LONG GONE*

*IT'S HARD BUT WE HAVE TO HOLD ON*

*TODAY PRESENTLY STANDS; TOMORROWS THEY*

*COME AND GO*

*BUT YESTERDAYS WILL REMAIN WITH US*

*THROUGHOUT OUR MINDS,*

*BODIES AND SOULS*

Four months into my pregnancy, my figure still looked the same, but Renee'?! Please! She was a whopper! Not so much her body, but her stomach was HUGE.

"Nish, the doctor said he thinks that I may be havin' twins," Renee spoke in a pitiful tone.

"Twins!" I was amazed by her statement.

VENOMOUS MINDS 2

"Yeah, they say that I'm carrying too big for someone who's almost 6½ months."

"So why are you crying?" I was confused.

"TWINS? What am I gonna do with twins?" she complained.

"Girl …twins are a blessing! Being able to have a baby is a blessing in itself…God only gives you what He knows that you can handle – RELAX! You'll manage!" I told her.

"Manage how? By myself? 'Cause Paul ain't shit. He's back to doing the same old shit, going back and forth to Virginia."

"Regardless of what HE does, YOU'LL make it! It might be hard, but you'll make a way. It's called strength and perseverance."

"Well I'm gonna need a lot of that," she said sadly.

POISON RUNNING FREE

"Speaking of doctor's appointment, I got a letter in the mail from the clinic. They gave me an appointment for next Thursday, but I was just there last Tuesday – it's too soon!" I argued.

"Did the letter say for what though?" Renee' asked.

"No it didn't; it just has the date and time, which is 9:00am."

"I have to go next Thursday too, because according to the doctor my ultrasound results will be back," Renee' explained.

"I guess I'll see you there then. And stop worrying yourself about the small things, because if you ARE pregnant with twins - what can you do about it?" I told her.

That following Thursday, Sandra and my mother took the trip with me to the clinic to see what this unplanned visit was all about.

VENOMOUS MINDS 2

"Nishelle Maron!" a woman called me. I stood up and followed her to the back. I had never been in this room before.

"Hello Nishelle, my name is Ms. Vandale and I am one of the counselors here at the Brownsville clinic. We called you back so soon because your results came back indicating that you have a venereal disease that's usually found in the blood. Sometimes doctors misdiagnose it thinking that it's a regular infection and simply treat it with antibiotics. Meanwhile, the disease is still present."

Lady please tell me that my baby's alright!

"Now the good thing is that the disease is treatable but slightly painful. It's a three week process and throughout these THREE CONSECUTIVE weeks, you are to come to the clinic once a week to receive an injection in the buttocks. Are you allergic to penicillin?"

"No."

POISON RUNNING FREE

"Good. Now you will be treated in this very same room and don't worry about signing in and waiting out front; just walk straight back and tell the nurse that you're here to see me."

Ms. Vandale was pleasant and very professional with breaking the news to me.

"What about my baby?" I asked nervously.

"The baby will be fine. As long as you get the THREE CONSECUTIVE treatments as I explained to you, the baby will be just fine," she assured me.

"But I mean are there any side effects or will this disease affect the baby in any way?" I rephrased my question. I needed to be sure that my baby was going to be okay.

"No there are no side effects and no it won't have any effect on the fetus. Your first injection will be today.

VENOMOUS MINDS 2

What the treatment does is it brings the level of the disease down to the point where it's undetectable and it also keeps you from infecting your mate. That's if he hasn't been infected yet. According to your blood count, you've had it for a long time now; your results were extremely high and right now you're at the tertiary stage which is the last stage."

Damn! My ass is saturated with this shit.

"What could have happened if it didn't show up?" I asked.

"Syphilis – depending on its stage, can cause several problems. It can do damage to your bones, skin, the nervous system and your heart," she explained.

"When you said long time, how long do you mean?"

POISON RUNNING FREE

I was now a 20 year old pregnant college dropout who was soaking in Syphilis. Damn! This is some serious bullshit! Could my mother have a done a better job raising me? Teaching me about the birds and the bees would have been a good start – but instead, she taught me how to roll my first joint then smoked it with me (at the age of twelve), instructed me on how to make cocaine sales, sent me to buy weed for her in her car that I shouldn't have been driving in the first place because I was only 14, pressured me into dating my first boyfriend AND, some several years later, to drop out of college so I could run her business that I wasn't even getting paid to do and all of this FOR WHAT??? Just to say that I know how it feels to be FUCKED?

"You're a level four, so this means you've had it for years. At the least, the past five years. Have you ever had any boils, minor cuts or bruises that excreted thick yellowish pus around your groin or genital area Nishi?" the counselor asked.

**VENOMOUS MINDS 2**

"No - but my first boyfriend did. He had them all the time and said that it was just a bump that had gotten infected," I explained to the counselor.

"Was he ever tested?" Ms. Vandale asked me.

"I don't know. He said his mother had given him some pills and just told him to take them until they were finished."

"Did the boils ever go away?" she asked.

"No. Well - after a while I think so. I'm not quite sure."

"Where is he now? Is he here with you?" the counselor frowned.

"No, we broke up YEARS ago."

"So he's not the father of your baby?"

"No."

POISON RUNNING FREE

"Okay, now that's another thing. In order for this treatment to work successfully and to avoid reinfection, the baby's father will have to come in for testing."

*Lord! How am I going to tell Teddy that he has to be tested for a disease that another man gave me?*

"Would he come to this same building?" I asked her.

"Yes, but he'll go across the hall. We don't treat men over here; this side is only for our prenatal patients," Ms. Vandale explained.

"Okay," I said softly.

*Damn man! I can't believe this shit. I seriously CAN NOT believe this shit is happening again.* I just kept thinking about my baby.

"Okay Nishelle, I have to tell you that the needle alone is scary – it's huge, but don't let that bother you," she said as she put on the latex gloves.

**VENOMOUS MINDS 2**

*A needle is the least that I'm thinking about right now lady.*

"I want you to pull up you skirt and bend over for me," she instructed.

With my nerves working the way that they were, I was hoping that I didn't shit on the poor woman.

"Mmm!" I moaned. Tears began to roll down my face as I hung over the metal chair. My past was haunting me once again.

"Okay Nishelle, you can stand up straight now."

As I stood up, I felt this throbbing pain in my left buttock area.

"What's wrong? Are you okay?" she asked. She saw the wetness on my face from crying.

"I just don't want anything to happen to my baby!" I began to cry again.

POISON RUNNING FREE

"Don't worry Nishelle. That's why we called you in, so we can take care of this situation now. I promise you, your baby's gonna be fine," she said, holding my hand as she consoled me.

"So - today is Thursday, which means I'll see you next Thursday at this time. Remember, it HAS to be done consecutively or else we'll have to start the treatment all over again," Ms. Vandale stressed.

"Okay," I said, giving her a half smile. The other half was in my ass and throbbing the shit out of me.

Renee' was the first person I saw as I entered the main waiting room.

"Hey Nish …is everything okay?" Renee asked, concern covering her face.

There were too many people in that room for me to even begin my story and plus, I just wanted to go home to rest. Depression slowly kicked in, but not to the point of me considering suicide like before.

"I'll call you later, okay?" I promised her and slowly turned to leave.

"Later Ree," Sandra said as she and my mother followed behind me.

"So Nish what did they say?" Sandra asked while we waited on the elevator to come.

"I'll tell you when we get in the van …Mommy can you drive?" I asked her as we entered the elevator.

"Okay."

After hopping my sore ass into the front passenger seat, I took a deep breath and told them everything.

"But Nish, is the baby gonna be alright?" Sandra asked.

"Yeah - as long as I get treated properly."

"Damn! I can't believe this shit! Oops! Sorry Gladys," Sandra covered her mouth.

"Well - I'm gonna ask Wasobi what he knows about it," my mother said.

Being that my uncle, Evelyn's husband, was studying to become a doctor, I guess she felt it necessary to shed some light on my situation. However, I didn't need any more light, 'cause right about now my life was, once again, at 5000 watts, and the last thing I wanted was for everyone to be all in my business.

"Ask him what? You don't have to ask him anything. The counselor already told me what I needed to do," I argued.

"Still - I wanna know," she insisted.

VENOMOUS MINDS 2

"Mommy, don't mention anything to Wasobi. I don't want people to know my business."

"Alright," she responded.

Too depressed and ashamed, I broke my promise and didn't call Renee'. I was tired of being interrogated. Plus, I had to figure out a way to explain all of this to Teddy...

\*\*\*\*\*\*

After that Friday's morning run, I called him up, knowing that MooMoo was in school.

"Hello?" Teddy answered the phone.

"Hey! It's me."

"I waved to you dis morning, didn't you see me?" he asked.

"No. Where at?"

POISON RUNNING FREE

"I was at dee light right across from Ebbets Field and you was picking up Ajaiwa," he described.

My mind was obviously someplace else because usually when and if we do pass one another while doing our routes, we acknowledge one another.

"Nah, I didn't see you. Listen...I need to talk to you. Are you stoppin' by later?" I asked.

"No, not tonight. I'll see you tomorrow though."

"Okay," I was satisfied with that.

"So how's me baby?" he inquired.

"Fine."

"What did you it (eat) today?" he asked.

"Nothing yet, but I'm gonna make me a salad sandwich when I hang up from you."

VENOMOUS MINDS 2

That's right....a salad sandwich. My locks were almost touching my shoulders now, and meat hadn't been a part of my diet for about three years now. Not long after my break up with Mike, I stopped eating beef, and eventually, I cut out chicken, eggs and milk; I hated milk; it gave me gas.

"So what are you gonna put on this sangwich (sandwich)?" Teddy then asked.

"Lettuce, tomato, cucumber, onions, a slice of cheese and some mustard AND that shit is going to be SO good. Anyway, let me go and make it now. If I don't see you during the run later then I'll see you tomorrow."

"No mit (meat)?" the possum eating foreigner then asked.

"Nah, I'm good!"

"Okay – take caye (care)!" Teddy said and hung up.

POISON RUNNING FREE

The following day I slept til 12:30 that afternoon. Those damn kids' were wearing me out.

"Ahh shit," I moaned as I turned to get out of bed. My ass was still killing me from the injection. I jumped in the shower, hoping that some hot water would do the trick and it did. I got dressed and headed downstairs to make myself something to eat.

"Hey Kyra baby! Wanna go outside? Come on!" Boom! Boom! Boom! My 100lb. Rottweiler hustled down the stairs. Grams had gotten rid of Champ, and as for Ginger - well, she died in the back yard beneath my mother's old orange van last summer. Rumor was that the husband of one of my mother's hang partners had poisoned my dog. BASTARD! He was another menace to society and the last I heard, he had gotten deported. For what? I don't know.

**VENOMOUS MINDS 2**

Kyra had been my baby for the past year or so and I took good care of her. From the day that I brought her home, she ate nothing but the best - Eukanuba. She took her vitamins daily and I fed her boiled eggs to keep her coat nice and shiny. Unlike her owner, she never had that long stringy cold in the corner of her eyes. Kyra was beautiful, but played a bit too much; if she ever ran into you, you'd definitely stumble – if not fall down.

"Here!" I threw her a piece of bread. I could see that someone had fed her already for me because the bag of food was sitting on the kitchen floor instead of where it should have been, in the broom closet.

"Now get out of my face. I don't feel like playing with you right now," I said, shooing her and opening the door to let her out back. While doing so the phone rang. *Somebody else is gonna have to answer that because my breakfast is calling me.*

POISON RUNNING FREE

RING! RING! RING! - RING! RING! RING! - RING! RING! R....

Dammit!

"Hello," I answered.

"Wow! I didn't think anyone was home. Where is everybody?" Evelyn asked.

"I guess no one's here because I just woke up not too long ago," I said.

"Well really I called to talk to you," Evelyn told me.

"Oh yeah? What's up?"

"I heard about what happened at the doctor's office the other day and I just wanted to say that I'm sorry to hear that. Back in our heydays (period of time) having Syphilis was like catching a cold. Almost everybody had it. But don't worry, because as long as you get treated you'll be fine."

VENOMOUS MINDS 2

"I know and I appreciate your concern and all, but how did you find out?"

"Your mother. She called here last night and spoke to Wasobi. They were on the phone for quite some time too. I was shocked, because I know how he feels about her. So when he hung up, I asked him what that was all about. He asked me if I knew that my niece had Syphilis. Of course, this was a shock to me and I said to myself, now why would Gladys tell Wasobi something like that? That's none of his business. I mean he's family and all, but some things are just personal," she expressed.

"EXACTLY! That's why I told her to keep her mouth shut," I angrily voiced.

What was her problem? My mother and I were like sisters. She was my friend. She was my world, so why would she reveal my physical health to the public when all I've ever done was protect her. Damn man!

POISON RUNNING FREE

"Nish. You there?" Evelyn asked.

"Yeah - I'm still here."

"I can tell you're a little upset, so I'm gonna let you go. If you ever need someone to talk to, you can call me okay?"

"Yeah," I said with tears rolling down my face.

Physically - I was strong, but deep down inside, my soul was weak. I just couldn't fathom why my mother would do such a thing even after I asked her not to.

I was the type of person that if someone harmed or tried to harm my family, I'd be the first to switch to DEFENSE MODE and was sure that my family would do the same for me. Was I missing something here? How can a person love you and yet hurt you at the same time?

"Sandra. Are you awake?" I said while chewing into the receiver. My salad sandwich was still to be devoured.

**VENOMOUS MINDS 2**

"Yeah - what's up?" she yawned.

"I called you to tell you this. Are you sure you're awake?" I asked again.

"Yeah! Yeah! Go on! I'm listening!" She seemed a bit more attentive now.

"I just hung up from Evelyn and do you know that my mother called Wasobi and told him everything?"

"Everything like what?" Sandra asked.

"Just like I said....EVERYTHING! They know what I got....how long I've had it. Like I said....everything!"

"WORD?! But you told her not to say anything."

"I guess she thought it was necessary to talk, regardless of how I felt."

POISON RUNNING FREE

"Nish - I don't know what to tell you. That's still your moms though and it's just a shame that you can't tell her anything in confidence."

"Anyway, I just called to tell you that. I'm gonna let you go back to sleep."

"Nah - it's okay `cause I have to get up soon anyway. I have to be to work by 3:00. Yo - did you tell Teddy yet?"

"Nah, he's coming over later and I plan to tell him then."

"Oh. Alright, so I'll call you later during the day," Sandra said.

"Okay, bye." I said.

"Later," she said and we hung up.

After hanging up, for a while I sat there just staring at my food. This is some real shit! Having lost my appetite, I picked at the edges of the bread.

VENOMOUS MINDS 2

RING! RING! RING!

"Shit. Who is it now?" I slowly got up to answer it.

"Hello," I said.

"Yo Nish - it's me again. Yo, you know I'm here for you right? If you ever need to get something off your chest, just give me a call. While taking my shower, I was thinking and seriously, that shit that your moms did was DEAD WRONG. You shouldn't have to stress over some shit that she's sayin'; you're already going through enough. So just keep your head up kid. It'll be alright. You hear me?" my friend to the end preached.

Of course, I started to cry. Obviously, the only true friend I had was Sandra.

"Yeah, I hear you."

"See now. Why you gotta start cryin.' I HATE this shit!" She began to cry too.

POISON RUNNING FREE

"I can't stand when people do dumb shit and not consider other people's feelings. Yo Nish, let me go and warm up my car, `cause the longer I stay on the phone with you, I'm just gonna keep cryin'. I'll talk to you later." CLICK! She quickly hung up.

Sandra and I were practically the same. We were both tomboys, we both loved our families to the point that we'd do almost anything for them and we were always the first ones to start crying. We could sense each other's feelings without saying a word. It was weird.

*******

"What's up?" Teddy greeted me as I opened the door for him. It was about 9:30 and he was smelling like a bag of weed.

"Nothing - I was just watching some T.V. up in my room."

"Why is dee house so dack (dark)?" he asked.

"I'm the only person here. My mother went upstate and my grandmother went to see her mother. She'll probably be home soon though," I responded.

Poppa was no longer with us, so every Saturday Grams would visit Granny to keep her company. I remember dropping her off at her Granny's house one Saturday morning.

"Nish you coming in right?" Grams turned and asked me.

"No. You know I'm not," I frowned.

"Why not?"

"Cause Grams you know that I don't like the smell of that house," I explained.

The house had a smell of bed pans and Bengay which was not my idea of an aromatic scent.

POISON RUNNING FREE

"Come on Nish....just for a few minutes," she begged.

I released a heavy sigh. "ONLY A FEW MINUTES!" I stressed.

As we approached the front door, what did we smell? SHIT. I started to fan. Grams found my actions to be hilarious.

"Who dat dere comin' through muh front doe?" Granny shouted from her bedroom.

"It's me - Mother! I got Nishi with me too," Grams announced.

"Oh okay. I just wanted to know, `cause I'm in here sittin' on the bucket. I been sittin' here for a while – I reckon it was sump'm (something) dat I eat," Granny explained.

VENOMOUS MINDS 2

The bucket was one of those large empty compound containers – aka, the ghetto porta potty.

I loved my great grandmother, but entering her house - I HATED it...

"Is Lee with you mudda?" Teddy asked as he removed his jacket.

"Yep." My senseless mother had taken my little brother upstate with her to meet Ethon.

"So what's up wid you? Didn't you have an appointment wid dee doctor on Turzday (Thursday)?"

"Yeah."

"So how's dee baby?" Teddy asked. I dropped my head and took a deep breath.

POISON RUNNING FREE

"That's what I wanna talk to you about." I slightly altered my seated position.

"What's wrong? Are you bleeding again?" he asked, worry lacing his voice...

\*\*\*\*\*\*\*

About a week after that episode in front of MooMoo's apartment building, it just so happened that I saw her again and finally got my chance to WHIP THAT ASS. Teddy tried hard to stop us and instead of grabbing her, he shoved me into a wall. Man, why did he do that? Sandra found a brick and threw it through his front passenger window; that night was a big mess. Two days later, I was seen in the emergency room and was told by the doctor that I was having a warning miscarriage...

"No – I'm not bleeding again, but the doctor found something in my blood."

"Like what?" he calmly asked.

"A counselor told me that it's a sexually trans....."
POW! He smacked me.

Now any other time, I would have hit him back.

"Teddy it's not my fault! I DIDN'T KNOW and she said as long as I get treated, the baby will be fine! Do you really think I wanted something like this to happen?" I explained.

"I never had any of those diseases and I didn't come to this country to get any either," he angrily stated.

I sat silently with a stinging left cheek, but this time I couldn't retaliate because I was totally to blame. I put his life on the line and I didn't wanna hurt him in any way.

"Teddy how do you think I felt when she told me? According to her, I had it for about five years....maybe more, which means I got it from Mike, my first boyfriend."

POISON RUNNING FREE

"And dis was the type of guy you choose to deal wid'," he disgustedly spat.

"Like I said - I didn't know and obviously, he was screwing around with someone else besides me," I said, looking away.

Man, was I feeling like shit at this point.

"So now what? Does this mean that I have it too?" Teddy asked.

"Not necessarily. She said that you should be tested just to make sure. This way if you are, I can't get re-infected," I explained. He stared at me real hard for about forty seconds. I thought he was going to hit me again, so I jumped at his slightest movement.

"Yeah - you need to jump," he sneered at me.

*Hmm! You don't know me you son of a bitch - you hit me again and I might just knock you the hell out.*

VENOMOUS MINDS 2

"So waye do I have to go?" he asked.

"To the same place I go for my regular check-ups, but only across the hall."

"Do I have to make an appointment?" Teddy seemed to be cooperating. This of course, made my life easier.

"No. She said that it's a walk-in site."

"We're goin' Monday morning, so make sure you're ready when I get haye," he ordered and immediately left...

Teddy tested negative - THANK GOD! My biggest fear was that he'd view me as a filthy human being and of course, I didn't want that.

\*\*\*\*\*\*

Several weeks had gone by, I was done with the treatments and things were back to normal again.

POISON RUNNING FREE

WHAAAAAMP! WHAAAAAMP!

He acknowledged me one morning as we did our route. I had just dropped off my last group at school and was heading for the gas station.

On the way to the gas station, I chose to take the route that would purposely cause me to pass by Teddy's apartment building. To my surprise, who did I see walking towards the corner grocery store? Although she had gained some weight, I still recognized her. Her clothes weren't at all fashionable and everything just seemed very bulky on the top. I don't remember her being top heavy. But wait a second.

I circled the block once, but by the time I made my way back around, MooMoo had already gone into the grocery store, so I parked up and waited.

When she came out, she crossed the street without even noticing me. Yep - just what I thought.

VENOMOUS MINDS 2

That afternoon on my way to pick up my 2:50 p.m. load, I saw Teddy at the air pump. He jumped as I pulled up alongside him and smiled when he realized that it was me.

"I see you need a new tire huh?" I stated as I stepped down out of my mother's van.

"Probably," he answered. Slowly, I walked closer to him as he covered the air valve.

"Dis is dee turd (third) time dis week I had to put air into dis same tire," Teddy stood up.

"So what else do you need to do?" I asked.

"Like what?" he questioned.

"What's up with you and Meryl …is she still telling you to get out?"

POISON RUNNING FREE

"She's still getting on me nerves, but if she wanna leave - then she can go, but I'm not livin' (leaving) me son," he explained.

"Oh...is that so? And you don't think you should be telling me anything else?"

"No."

"Is Meryl pregnant Teddy?" I got to the point.

"No," Teddy answered.

"She's not?"

"No," He repeated.

POW! I smacked him dead in his face.

"You're a FUCKING liar!" I screamed. "I saw her this morning on my way to the gas station. She was going to the store at the corner of your block."

Teddy looked around and then held his head down.

VENOMOUS MINDS 2

"Nishi I didn't want to tell you because you were already goin' tru (through) a lot. You almost had a miscarriage and I knew that if you found out about she - it would bahduh (bother) you," he elaborated.

"YOU let me be the judge of that. I thought you were looking for your own place."

"Me was, but I couldn't find anyting. She asked me dee same ting and I told she dat if she really didn't want me around to leave and to take she sister wid she too, but to leave me son though."

"Oh and she JUST so happened to get pregnant again!" I spat.

"Nishi she told me that she was pregnant about a munt (month) after you told me that you were pregnant."

"How convenient - she gets pregnant again and you go nowhere."

"Believe me Nishi. I didn't want this gyul to get pregnant again and according to she, she didn't want to either."

"So what now?" I asked the liar.

"I'll see you later, `cause it's already 2:47pm," he terminated our discussion.

Now that MooMoo was pregnant too, it was going to be a long, hot ass summer.

"You make me sick!" I yelled from my mother's van.

I'm so sick of all this shit! I can't wait until school is finished. Two weeks HURRY UP and come!

"Nishi, I'll stop by you later, o.k.?" he yelled back.

I started the van, quickly threw it in drive and skidded off. MooMoo was forever killin' the mood!

VENOMOUS MINDS 2

\*\*\*\*\*\*\*\*\*\*\*\*\*\*\*\*\*\*\*\*\*\*\*\*\*\*\*\*\*

# To Be Continued

# About The Author

Nichole Martin, author of the Venomous Minds series lives in New York with her children and other family members. She is a very active advocate for victims of Domestic Violence, having giving many interviews and motivational speeches on the subject. Speaking to women and groups nationally to bring awareness to the plight of Domestic Violence victims and survivors, as well as having constant contact and communications with the White House on this most important issue. She also still loves riding a motorcycle!

## Author Nichole Martin

**POISON RUNNING FREE**

www.ingramcontent.com/pod-product-compliance
Lightning Source LLC
Chambersburg PA
CBHW071145170626
46809CB00002B/781